Greg's Fourth Adventure in Time

C. M. Huddleston
2018

Greg's Fourth Adventure in Time

Published by:
Interpreting Time's Past PRESS
Crab Orchard, Kentucky

For information address:
Interpreting Time's Past, LLC,
450 Old Richmond Road, South
Crab Orchard, KY 40419

Cover by Jeanine Henning
Front Cover, Wagon with oxen,
   by Pearson Scott Foresman
Wagon (p. 228) Gates Frontiers Fund Wyoming
   Collection within the Carol M. Highsmith Archive,
   Library of Congress, Prints and Photographs Division

ISBN: 978-0-9964304-8-7

For my best first reader ever,
my grandson -
Ethan Harrison Davis

The home is the child's first school,
the parent is the child's first teacher,
and reading is the child's first subject.
First Lady Barbara Bush

Chapters

1
Grounded

"Mom, I can either die accidentally or from sheer boredom! Seriously, you're grounding me for a whole month of absolutely no time travel? Are you serious?" I shouted as I left Mom's office, slammed the door, and headed to my room at the other end of our sprawling ranch house.

"Greg, Greg! Wait," called Rose, following close on my heels.

"NO, I WILL NOT WAIT," I shouted as I fell across my bed in a huff, only to be licked across the face and behind both ears by Boone, whom I had awoken from his morning nap.

"Greg, your Mom is only worried about you because of the Pirate. Don't you realize how anxious she becomes when you go off alone in time? I know a month of no time travel will be hard, but she did warn you," Rose stated in a pretty good imitation of Mom Nellie, our housekeeper and second mom.

Now I guess you might be fairly confused right about now, coming in on the middle of yet another fight between Mom and me. It's not like we have them often, but ever since the Pirate kidnapped Rose and me, threatened Mom, and generally created havoc in our lives, Mom has been super protective. *Like a grizzly bear with two cubs threatened by a pack of wolves* is how Dad describes her current state.

I mean really? Really? It seems to me Rose and I handled the situation with the Pirate pretty well—we escaped (okay, I got shot, but it was only a flesh wound), met Theodore Roosevelt (way cooler than it sounds), found and rescued Mom (who had been stabbed), and left the Pirate unconscious in the wilds of North Dakota at some unknown time in the past with what appeared to be absolutely no way to return to our time.

Still confused? Sorry. Short version. Rose and I plus my parents, Ken and Emily Harrison, and Nellie and James Jackson, all live in far western North Dakota (at least for now), and we are all TTIs—Time Traveling Individuals (you know, *humans who are born with the time-travel gene*). Rose's father, Matthew Engram, who can also time travel, is a logician, and is on his way home from Africa, where he worked for the government, and will live here with us. That's why Rose has been living with us. Did I tell you the house is huge? My Dad (Ken Harrison) and James work for the STTIU (the Smithsonian Time Travel Investigative Unit). Nellie, our second mom, housekeeper, cook, and home school instructor, writes novels and has published several. And then there is Mom (Emily Harrison), not your typical mom, as mine happens to be an archaeologist. Her work is why we live in North Dakota. She's excavating at the Theodore Roosevelt National Park, about an hour from here. We've lived in lots of places before now.

I'm Greg Harrison, age 14, tall for my age, already six feet, home schooled, and this is my fourth narrative about my time travel adventures. Rose, also 14, time jumped with me several times last year, including our great adventure with the Pirate. She writes parts of my narratives as she claims being a girl makes her a more *descriptive* writer. Oh, yeah, I'd better tell you about the Pirate. No one knows his real name, but he's an evil, time-jumping thief of historic artifacts. Dad's job is to catch him and turn him over to the STTIU. The Pirate stands about 6'2" and has dark, almost black hair, and wears an eye patch—hence his nickname.

Okay, what have I left out? I guess you need to know why I am *in trouble* and grounded. You see, recently, I've time traveled back into the past several times to see if I can find the Pirate's body. I know exactly where we left him. He wasn't dead, just knocked senseless. We left him somewhat defenseless in Indian country in the 1800s. I mean, I figure either he starved, died of thirst, or met with predators, either human or animal. I just want to make sure he can't or won't return. So, I have used the Pirate's Bowie knife to jump back and see if I can figure out what happened to him. I am always armed and have my trusty steed Cody for quick getaways. Besides, I can always just jump back to our time. I don't know why Mom is freaking out. She even had the nerve to tell me she'd prefer I died of boredom!

REALLY?

"Greg, you're most likely jumping back into the mid-to-late 1800s when the Plains Indians ruled this area. No wonder your Mom is worried. You might find the Pirate, but you also might find the Sioux or even the Blackfeet. Or they might find you," Rose reminded me. "I think you'd better just settle down for the rest of the summer and think about our coming trip before Emily makes you stay behind."

"Sure, why not," I murmured. "I'll vegetate here and die of boredom while you and your Dad go off on vacation."

"Don't start. I haven't seen Dad in over a year, and we need to reconnect. That's the only reason we're taking this trip. I'll be back before you know it."

And, just like a girl, she twirled about and marched back down the hallway toward the other end of the house and her bedroom. Over the sound of her footsteps (she's wearing her usual cowboy boots), I heard Dad's plane land on our private strip and considered going out to meet him. But I was still too mad. Besides, once Mom has told him about my going off again, he will probably ground me for another month.

Rose, on the other hand, would not be grounded in boring North Dakota. Rose's father, Matthew, planned to fly into New York City. They intended to spend a week or so together there before returning here to live. We have plenty of room in this old rambling log ranch house. Even with Mom and Dad having offices, Mom's laboratory, the schoolroom, and such, we still have about five empty rooms. Mom's excavations will continue for at least another season or two as she can only excavate for about five months each year. No reason for us to move on to yet another dig site. I hope we can stay here for a long time. Even if it is boring.

Later that morning, I heard someone tap quietly at my door. "Greg, before I leave, I have to tell you something. Please open your door," Rose whispered.

"No," I answered.

"It's about the Pirate, now open up, or I'll blow this door down."

Laughing, I got up and opened my door to confront Rose, and discovered a 5'2" girl dressed in, believe it or not, a lavender dress and strappy sandals instead of her usual jeans and cowboy boots. Yes, there stood Rose, but not the Rose I knew.

"Why are you dressed like that? And what's this about blowing my door down?" I asked.

"I needed to get your attention, and that's what came to mind. Now, shut up and listen," she answered with more than some attitude. "I overheard Ken tell Emily that he and James saw the Pirate in San Francisco yesterday. Yes, they're sure; so he's alive and back in our time. Ken's perturbed that you disobeyed your Mom and went out looking for the Pirate again. So, keep quiet, and stay out of trouble. I gotta go, but I wanted you to know before you decided to do something stupid."

"Hey, I never do stupid things—reckless, careless, even foolish, but never stupid," I stated as she walked away. "Hey, nice dress."

I think she mumbled something about *boys* before waving over her shoulder and joining James at the front door. He planned to drop her at the Denver airport to meet her flight to New York before picking up supplies we needed at the ranch. I'd planned to go along, but Mom had squashed that idea. Part of my grounding—no flying either.

Being grounded didn't mean I didn't have to do my chores, so I headed to the barn to feed the horses. Boone bounced along beside me. I know it's his way of being excited, but Australian Shepherd puppies seem to bound more than *walk* from one spot to the next. Boone, named for my heroes Daniel and Squire Boone, will soon be a year old, but I expect he'll be about ten before he settles down. As I walked toward the corral, he slipped under the fence and started to try herding our horses. Accustomed to Boone's tactics, or would that be *antics*, they just kept grazing and ignored his barking until he began nipping at their fetlocks.

"Boone, come," I shouted over the noise of him barking and the horses neighing and stomping.

Reluctantly, he joined me at the barn door and took to chasing the barn cat, who was smart enough to climb into the loft. I had filled the hamper and was moving from stall to stall when Dad appeared in the doorway.

"Greg, we need to talk."

"I know, Dad. I know I should not have disobeyed Mom. Sorry."

"Okay, apology accepted, but you're still grounded. However, well, I mean, well. . . .we need to talk."

This sounded ominous. "Sure, okay."

"Greg, the Pirate is alive. James and I saw him in San Francisco."

"Yeah, Rose told me before she left. She overheard you and Mom talking."

"Well, we couldn't catch him, and we've no idea of how he escaped the past. I thought since you are so anxious to find him, you might like to help me try to figure out how. No, don't interrupt. I have your Mom's permission to take you along since I need your help jumping the horses back in time, but you'll have to promise to follow each and every command I give you without question. Can you do that?" he asked, giving me his *I mean it* stare.

"Yes, sir. I promise. When will we go?" I answered.

"First thing tomorrow morning. Now finish your chores and make sure our horses and all our tack are ready and in good repair. I'll see to the firearms and other supplies. We'll plan to be gone all day, but will return to our time each night." Dad smiled at me and then walked back toward the house, turning at the edge of the corral to tell me, "Oh, we're not taking Boone. Can't risk him not being close if we need to time jump, or barking and making our presence known." After a bit more discussion, Dad returned to the house, leaving me to finish my chores.

"Yes! Yes! Yes!" I shouted to myself, pumping my fist in the air after Dad was out of sight. My uncommon ability to take animals with me when I time jump meant I got to go on a mission with Dad. Fantastic!

"Come on, Boone, let's feed the horses," I called, suddenly feeling much better about the whole situation.

2
Searching for the Pirate

Dad and I packed up our gear right after dawn the next morning. I could tell the day would be a hot one. Considering it was only the beginning of June, I hadn't expected the heat to arrive so early in the summer. Dad carried two rifles and two pistols out to the corral, and I carried our saddle bags that Nellie'd packed with sandwiches and other goodies for our trip. In case we didn't make it back before dark, we also had sleeping bags and *heat-and-serve* stuff for supper.

Mom followed us out, looking anxious. "Ken, do you think this is wise? I mean, what difference does it make how he got back to our time?" she asked.

"Emily, we need to know if he's working alone or has a partner. Greg and I will be careful. We can both jump back to our time if we encounter any danger, plus we have the rifles and pistols, which I am sure we won't need. Relax. We'll either return later today or call about dusk to let you know we are back in our time. I have the satellite phone. I'll even check in with you during the day."

"But Ken, the sat phone only works in our time . . ."

"Emily, go to work. Concentrate on your excavations and let me do my job. Now off with you," Dad joked, and grabbing the reins I held out, leapt gracefully into Romeo's saddle, bowed at the waist, and threw Mom a kiss. He can be so silly! Rose calls him *romantic!*

It took several minutes for us to situate each of the saddlebags and rifles. We placed the pistols in saddle holsters where we could reach them easily. Dad wrapped the sat phone and placed it in a leather bag he wore strapped to his chest. I, of course, had my cell phone, but with coverage being so spotty out here, it would likely not be useful, except as a camera. We set off, only to have to return to the house and hand Boone over to Nellie for safe keeping. We could hear him barking and her telling him to hush all the way past the barn and out onto the prairie.

"Greg, take us directly to the spot where you left the Pirate. You did remember the Pirate's Bowie knife?" Dad asked.

"Sorry," I shouted as I raced Cody back to the house, grabbed the knife, and rejoined Dad. Of course, that set Boone off once again.

We rode for about two hours. I knew where the incident had taken place. When we arrived, I took hold of Dad's reins and the Bowie knife and time jumped right back to the spot in time when Mom and I had left the Pirate, naked and unconscious. (Guess you should know, actual *time jumping* is not some dramatic event, like in the movies. TTIs simply grab onto an historic artifact and allow our consciousness to take us to that time. It happens in an instant.)

Guess I also better explain why we left him naked. You see, if he'd had any item on him, even a piece of clothing, from another time, he could jump to the time when that item was made. By leaving him naked, stark naked, Mom and I thought he would be stranded in time. Now, some of you might wonder why we didn't turn him over to the authorities and charge him with all his crimes. We could have, but it's hard to keep a time traveler in jail or any type of confinement. All they have to do is find one item, any item, from another time, and they can jump to that time and will most likely escape. Now, we could have brought him back to the ranch so Dad and James could have taken him back to the STTIU, but that created another set of problems. Mom was injured (remember I said the Pirate stabbed her?), and we were short one horse. We could have made him walk, but keeping an eye on him and traveling that slowly would have meant another night on the trail. Besides, he was unconscious, thanks to Rose. So Mom and I left him naked and out cold, back in time, and unable to escape. Or so we'd thought. (Oh, I explained all of this in my narrative, *Greg's Third Adventure in Time*.)

"Greg, let's ride in wide-ranging circles from here and look for anything out of place."

"Uh, Dad, I've already done that twice and found not one trace of him. Nothing," I replied. "So, that might be a waste of time. I'd planned, before Mom grounded me, to look for nearby water holes and streams. I figured the first thing he would seek would be water. Right?"

"Makes sense," Dad replied, pulling out a topographic map of the area, showing most of the nearby streams and watering holes.

We surveyed the map for several minutes, marking each likely waterhole and stream with a red circle. "How about we try all the ones to the east first and then work clockwise from there?" he suggested.

"Okay by me," I replied.

The day dragged on and on under a hot sun. We found the first two watering holes marked on the map to be bone dry. The first stream had some barely moving, nasty-looking water. Dad and I worked our way first upstream for several miles and then turned downstream and searched both banks. Nothing. After a quick lunch in the saddle, we turned southwest toward a small stream marked right at the edge of our topo. Dad led the way. About mid-afternoon, Dad and I both heard wolves howling somewhere to our left over a small rise. Wolves howl differently than coyotes. We approached on foot, leading our horses. Creeping to the top of the hill, we soon spotted three wolves circling something on the ground. Dad pulled out his binoculars, scanned the area, and then, grabbing his reins from me, mounted and rode swiftly toward the wolves.

Wolves will usually back off when a person approaches and these did. Not far, though, so our horses spooked, making them hard to control. I ended up mounting Cody and leading Dad's gelding, Romeo (Mom named him). I found Dad tending to a small unconscious (I hoped he wasn't dead) American Indian boy.

"Looks like he was thrown from a horse. There's a lump on his head, and his arm is broken. Hand me my canteen," Dad instructed.

We worked for several minutes doing general first aid stuff, like sheltering him from direct sunlight, forcing water between his lips, and looking for any other injuries.

"Greg, see if you can find me two, or even three, straight branches about a foot long. You might need to ride back to that last stream to find trees. If you encounter trouble, get off a shot before you jump. I'll take cover, if I can find any. Otherwise, I'll be right here."

I handed Dad his reins and mounted quickly. Cody seemed to sense the urgency in my actions and reached a full gallop with little urging. I guess the search took about a half hour, and when I returned, I found Dad in a bit of difficulty. The boy had awakened, the wolves had returned, and Dad sat surrounded by fifteen angry-looking American Indian men. I had no idea what tribe.

Stay calm—Mom's mantra for any situation in our time or in the past—*and use your intelligence.* Instead, I rode straight down the hill toward Dad, dismounted, and handed him the two sturdy straight sticks. Next, I reached for my saddlebag and pulled out my extra shirt and the Bowie knife. That might have been a mistake, as two of the Indian men shouted and gestured. So I held up the knife and the shirt and turned toward one of the calmer men. Then, I cut the shirt and began tearing it into strips, tossing each to Dad.

Now this would never have worked had those Indians been Sioux or any of the most war-like tribes. They watched as Dad placed the splints on the boy's arm. Still holding the knife, I couldn't move to help him hold the splints and tie them in place. Dad motioned for one man to help. Soon, one Indian sat holding the boy, while another held the splints in place, and Dad secured the arm. All seemed to proceed well until the wolves got too close to the Indian's horses which were held by an Indian boy about my age. Before I knew what was happening, one man pulled up his rifle and shot toward the wolves. I had dropped Cody's reins while cutting the shirt, and Dad had let Romeo wander while tending the boy. Both horses took off. Wolves scattered. The boy cried out, and Dad cursed loudly.

Soon after everyone settled back down, Dad had the boy's arm splinted. Then, before we knew what was happening, the Indians mounted up, took the boy, and rode off, leaving us stranded. No horses.

"Well Greg, which way would you like to walk?" Dad asked with a chuckle.

"Toward our horses?"

"Sounds like a plan."

We had walked about an hour, following their trail, when we approached another stream and found not only our horses, but the remains of a camp. A stone fire ring held ashes and several burnt food cans. Burnt, twenty-first-century food cans.

"Looks like the Pirate camped here in this time," Dad surmised.

"But why camp in the past?" I asked.

"I guess so no one would find him, but he was taking quite a risk camping in Indian territory. Looks like he brought food from the present. I guess his Bowie knife served as his artifact to the past."

"Let's jump back and look at his camp in our time," I suggested.

After rounding up Cody and Romeo, Dad and I jumped back to 2016 and found a much different-looking camp. We could tell the Pirate had been camping there for at least a week, based on the junk he left behind. Dad gathered it all up and placed the smaller items in a garbage bag we had brought along. The Pirate had left behind food containers, a water bag, a small cooler, and two sleeping bags. We'd come back later and clean up the mess.

"Two sleeping bags," Dad stated.

"Yep, he has a partner," I said. "I guess he walked to his camp when we left him, and then his partner found him there. Short one horse, I guess they figured to leave all this behind."

"Could be, maybe . . ., on the other hand, perhaps both camps had a sleeping bag, and he used it to jump back to the present and left it here. Or, he could have jumped from that camp using one of the food cans. Let's look for any other evidence of a partner," Dad suggested.

We spent the rest of the day searching the immediate area in both the past and the present. Nothing. We found no trail to follow and no other evidence. So, only a bit wiser, Dad and I returned home, much to Mom's relief.

I was still grounded.

3
Matthew Engram Comes Home

"James, I don't need someone to fly with me or meet me at the gate. I'm 14 and can find my way to Daddy's gate for his arrival. After I arrive in New York, I have an hour. I plan to eat, go to the bathroom, and wait. I don't need a chaperone," I pleaded.

"Sorry, Rose. Since the thing with the Pirate, the STTIU insists all TTI minors traveling alone have a chaperone, especially you and Greg."

"All right, but I am not sitting with someone on the plane. *Whoever* can follow me when I get off the plane, but I'm going to ignore them completely. Is that clear?"

"Sure thing, Rose. You've always been stubborn. And I won't tell Nellie, or she'll be calling and giving you a piece of her mind. Now, give me a big hug and get on board," James answered.

I felt relieved that James had escorted me to the gate for my flight. Ever since the Pirate kidnapped me and Greg, I've been a little nervous. Besides, well,

James and Nellie are like my second parents. I've known them since I was tiny. Now that we all live at the Harrisons' ranch, I have grown even closer to them. Nellie and James have had legal responsibility for me ever since Dad left for Africa. Ken and Emily Harrison do also, but Nellie and James helped raise me. I've always called Nellie, *Mom Nellie*, as I didn't want Daddy to think I had replaced my real mom by calling Nellie *Mom*. Does that make sense? Since I still had Daddy, I just called James, *James*, but he was always a second father.

During the flight, I finished a fantasy book by my new favorite author Patricia Reding and would have started the sequel, but didn't have it on my Kindle yet. So instead, I started reading a rctclling of *Beauty & the Beast* by Rebecca Hammond Yager. Amazing! Nellie's always telling me about books her friends have written. By the time the plane landed at JFK, I was engrossed in the story. I grabbed a chicken wrap and a drink, found the exit from Customs, and settled back down to read and wait. Yes, I noticed the smartly dressed woman following me everywhere, but I ignored her.

Daddy's plane from London arrived right on schedule. He must have made it through Customs in record time, because before I knew it there he was! I flew into his arms, giving him a big hug, as he walked out the door. I hadn't seen him in ages. He was tanned, smiling, carrying several shopping bags, and pulling his suitcase. I took the handle from him, and off we walked.

We spent the next few days touring all the important sights in New York City: the Statue of Liberty, the Empire State Building, Ellis Island and the Immigration Museum, the Metropolitan Museum of Art, and the 9/11 Memorial. We stayed at the ritzy The Pierre hotel, right on Central Park. We went to Times Square at night to see the lights and took in two Broadway shows—*Hamilton* and *Chicago*. We even shopped. Daddy needed clothes for North Dakota. I don't want to brag, but Daddy spent a fortune on our stay.

We had just returned from a long walk in Central Park when I broached my idea, something I had been thinking about for weeks. "Daddy, I know you'd planned for us to go straight back to the Harrisons' ranch, but well, I was hoping we could make a slight side trip?"

"Ah, and what would this side trip entail? Time-travel?"

"Well, yes, but not from here. From Rochester, New York," I stated firmly but with enthusiasm. "We could ask the STTIU for some clothing and an artifact for 1885, and then make a leisurely drive to Rochester."

"Why in the world would you want to visit Rochester in 1885?"

"Okay. You see. Well, I think I told you about Greg and me finding the trunk in the attic with all the Wild West show costumes. Then, after our adventure, I read up on the shows and found out about Annie Oakley. So, I read a biography about her and one about William Frederick Cody—you know, Buffalo Bill."

"Yes, I know who Buffalo Bill is, but why Rochester?"

"Oh, the Sioux Chief Sitting Bull first performed in the show on June 15th in Rochester. We could see him, Buffalo Bill, and Anne Oakley in their first ever appearance together!" I finished my explanation and waited for Daddy to answer.

"I'll think about it. For now, go relax and think about what you want for dinner."

So, I watched television, finished my book, and wondered if I was going to Rochester. Daddy made me wait until the end of our Indian curry dinner before giving me his answer.

"Rose, this is the 13th. We don't have time for a *leisurely* drive to Rochester. . ."

"Ah . . . Daddy . . . " I started to complain when he interrupted me.

"So I changed our flights, and we leave in the morning for Rochester and will fly back to Denver from there. Appropriate clothing and an 1885 artifact are being delivered to our room while we are out. You'll need to find us a hotel room and transportation in Rochester when we're finished eating. I have to call in to check on things in Africa and to make sure the transfer of duties is being accomplished to my satisfaction."

By bedtime, I had booked a hotel room in Rochester and had a car reserved at the airport. I'd even printed a map to our hotel from the airport and had an idea where on Driving Park Avenue the Rochester Driving Park had been located in the previous century. I'd researched the Rochester Driving Park, and discovered it had been Rochester's fairgrounds, and had hosted horse races and all types of events in the previous century, including Buffalo Bill's Wild West show. My research revealed many things about the park, such as how a fire destroyed two of the park's grandstands in 1899. In the early 1900s, the park hosted auto races and several three-ring circuses before becoming home to a band of Romany, better known as Gypsies. In November of 1902, one of the Romany girls performed the "Hoochie-Coochie" and incited a riot! Anyway, the park's site is now a housing community, so I had to spend a great deal of time finding a nearby place where Daddy and I could park and jump back to 1885. Thank heavens the website provided a map of the area!

On the morning of the 15th, in our hotel in Rochester, Daddy and I dressed in snappy 1880's clothing. I had a fitted cotton-print bodice with a draped cotton-serge skirt that fell to just below the tops of my laced ankle boots. I also had a straw hat with a ribbon matching the color of my dress. I carried a sunshade, or parasol, to keep the sun off. Daddy, on the other hand, looked dapper in his white shirt, waistcoat (vest), and narrow fitting jacket. He had a paisley tie and sported pin-striped pants. Across his waistcoat lay his watch fob. He even had a Derby style hat. The STTIU costume department had sent the wrong size shoes, so Daddy just wore his new black cowboy boots. We dressed and left the hotel in plenty of time. After parking near the site, we checked for passersby and jumped. We landed next to the road to the Driving Park.

Off we walked on our next great adventure.

4
Annie Oakley

Daddy and I arrived early and wandered the park for a while, looking at all the animals and props. Buffalo Bill's show used several hundred animals, mostly horses, but also some mules and burros, American bison, and even longhorn cattle. Near the entrance gate sat a stage coach, several rough-looking wagons, a surrey, and three Prairie Schooner wagons, all of which looked very out of place in New York state. We watched as various cowboys, Mexican rancheros, American Indians, buffalo hunters, dance hall girls, pioneer women, and soldiers passed by. Nearly an hour had passed with us gawking about when Daddy reached in his pocket and pulled out a cardboard pass reading "Press" with St. Louis *Herald* printed below.

"So, ready to meet Annie Oakley?" he asked quietly.

"Truly?"

"Yes, it's all arranged. Come on. Let's find her tent."

I knew all about Annie. Born in Ohio, in 1860, Phoebe Ann Oakley Mozee, called Annie even as a young girl, had grown up in an extremely poor family. Living in a log cabin, her parents and the seven siblings, all girls except one, struggled to survive. When Annie was only four, her father, returning from selling their grain and other farm produce at the market, was caught in an early winter ice storm and returned home frozen. He never walked again and died in March of the following year. In subsequent years, Annie's mother moved her children to a smaller cabin and tried to make ends meet. She lost one daughter to tuberculosis, and the others often went hungry until Annie learned to wander the surrounding forest with her father's Kentucky long rifle, hunting for game. Soon Annie provided all the meat for the family's table.

After her mother remarried and they moved yet again, Annie was removed from the home and taught to read and write and do needlework at the County Infirmary, which was kind of like an orphanage. From there, Annie moved to a homestead to help a young family, where she was imprisoned, made to do all the household work, and starved. They wouldn't allow her to contact her family. Her story of hardship continued, even after she escaped and returned to the County Infirmary. Only as a young teen did Annie finally return to her family, where she once again provided for their welfare. Annie's shooting abilities and understanding of hunting strategies bagged so much game that she created her own little business, shipping great hampers of quail and such game to market and to hotels in Cincinnati.

As Daddy and I walked, I remember the story of how she met Frank Butler and bested him in a shooting contest in Cincinnati when she was only fifteen years old. A marksman and showman who traveled from town to town, Frank Butler often challenged local celebrities to shooting contests as part of his show. In Cincinnati, a hotel keeper and client of Annie's bet $100 that Annie could out-shoot the famous Frank Butler. Annie and her siblings even placed $50 of their own money on her. Twenty-five times she brought down the target, with the referee calling "Dead" each time. Frank Butler only managed twenty four.

Enamored of the young slim girl who had beaten him, Frank Butler began writing letters to Miss Annie Oakley. Having seen Frank's show, Annie trained herself to shoot faster, do tricks, and hit impossible targets. Frank wooed her with letters and gifts. The following year they married. Soon Annie appeared in his shows. Then she became the star, and Frank gladly settled into the background as her agent. Between shows, when possible, Annie attended school and educated herself. By 1885, she and Frank worked for Buffalo Bill Cody, the West's greatest showman.

Turns out, Annie Oakley's tent was easy to find. Her name, printed on a banner, hung over the door, and outside stood three men smoking large cigars and talking loudly. Right next to Annie's tent sat an even larger one with "Col. William Frederick Cody" printed above the door. I already knew from reading her biography that Annie had her own tent, and it usually sat near Buffalo Bill's tent. As Daddy and I approached, we could hear the men's conversation.

"As I have stated before, we must have new cabinet cards to sell. I sent for our photographer, but Chief Sitting Bull refuses to pose for a photograph until he can do so with Annie," stated a sharply dressed man.

Colonel Cody, better known as Buffalo Bill, answered, "I'll speak with him, Nate, and assure him Little Missy desires the photograph as well. When can she be ready? .... Wait, instead, Major, you ask Annie to be ready in about an hour for a photograph with the chief. If we can get them together before today's show, we might have the cards ready for our next tour stop." And off he walked in the direction of the Indian encampment.

"Daddy," I whispered, "the man on the left is Nate Salisbury, Buffalo Bill's business manager. The one on the right must be Major John M. Burke, his press agent. I read about them in Annie's biography."

"Right, now follow my lead."

"Pardon me, might one of you gentlemen be Major Burke?" Daddy asked as we approached.

"Yes, sir, may I help you?" Major Burke replied.

"Mr. Matthew Engram, St. Louis *Herald*, here to interview Miss Oakley. My paper sent you a telegram requesting an interview. This is my daughter, Rose. I hope it is not an inconvenience. She's a big fan of Miss Oakley's and begged to come along to see the show."

"No, no inconvenience at all. Everything is set. Little Missy loves her fans. You will have about three-quarters of an hour with Miss Oakley; however, I need to have a few words with her first, if you don't mind."

At that, he loudly called her name, and when she responded, he stepped quickly into the tent, setting off a ruckus of barking.

"That would be George, their French poodle," I explained. "He's part of the show."

Major Burke returned promptly with a tall, distinguished man at his side. I knew right off, he was Annie's husband, Frank Butler.

"Annie will be right with us, Mr. Engram. Please remember, she only has a limited time." Then calling for George, who ran to his side, he and Major Burke strolled away.

Annie Oakley stepped from her tent and pulled the front panels back and tied them at opposite posts. Inside sat a lovely walnut rocking chair and a side table piled with books. Beside it, in a basket, I could see some intricate needlework in a hoop and skeins of silk and wool thread. Her biography had mentioned she loved to do needlework and to read. On the ground lay several colorful woven carpets. Stools, a bicycle, George's food and water dishes, two cots, and various bits of clothing were all neatly arranged or hung on hat stands and various hooks.

Little Missy, as Buffalo Bill always called her, turned out to be a tiny, twenty-five-year-old woman, maybe 110 pounds, slender and barely more than five feet tall in her boots. Dressed in a light brown doeskin, tight-fitting bodice and matching skirt that ended in a thick, deep fringe and fell to just above her boot tops, she looked like many of the cabinet cards I had seen of her. A kerchief and a boiled wool cowboy hat hung nearby, all she needed to be ready for her photography session with Sitting Bull.

"Sir, could you please pull up two stools for you and your daughter?" Annie asked Daddy, while pulling her rocking chair out onto a rush mat that lay before the tent.

Then she turned and took my hand in hers and introduced herself. "Good afternoon, I'm Annie. I was just catching up on some reading and understand you are a big admirer. How can I help you today?"

"Mrs. Oakley..." I began.

"No, just Annie," she interrupted.

"I'm Rose Engram, and I had no notion of meeting you today. I thought we were only here to take in the show, but if I might ask. How can I improve my aim?" I asked brazenly. I heard Daddy let out a little gasp behind me.

"Oh, you shoot? Rifles or pistols, or both?" she asked.

"Either," I replied.

Daddy whispered, "We'll discuss this little secret later."

"How about we do a bit of shooting, and then I can see how to help you?" Annie suggested, turned, and began gathering up a satchel and several firearms right as Frank Butler returned with George.

We all followed on her heels as she led us into the empty grandstand and occupied a table that sat near the gate. Before I knew what was happening, Annie Oakley handed me a rifle and asked me to take aim at a target already positioned several yards away. I steadied the rifle, aimed, and took my shot. High! Just like always. Greg teases me about only being able to hit targets more than six feet tall, and then only the tops of their heads.

Almost half an hour passed with Annie instructing me in how to hold the rifle and aim properly, how to pull the rifle up quickly and aim, and even how to fire a shotgun. She turned out to be a wonderful teacher, and I improved rapidly. Before I knew it, she introduced us to Chief Sitting Bull, Nate Salisbury, and Colonel Cody. I asked Colonel Cody for an autograph. He and Annie signed cabinet cards for me. I planned to keep Annie's, but decided to give Colonel Cody's to Greg for Christmas. Chief Sitting Bull said little, but clapped and smiled each time Little Missy hit a target.

After watching the photography session, Annie taught me a few tricks about shooting and promised more lessons if I wanted to return. By that time, Daddy and I had to say our goodbyes and walk toward the grandstands for the afternoon show. We had excellent seats. Buffalo Bill himself opened the show, riding in on his big white horse and introducing us all to his Wild West. All those participants Daddy and I'd seen earlier carried out stage coach robberies, roped cattle and buffalo, fought Indians, twirled ropes, rode wild horses, shot rifles and pistols, and entertained us for over two hours.

Just as all the newspapers once reported, Annie was the star. The audience gasped, cheered, and applauded throughout her performance. She shot glass balls that were thrown into the air before she even reached for her rifle. Once she broke four thrown at the same time after changing for a different double-barreled gun in the middle of the feat. George, their French poodle, sat calmly on a stool, and she shot objects off his head. He didn't even flinch. She shot another target while viewing its reflection in a Bowie knife to set her aim. She shot from horseback. She shot at a full run. She moved quickly from stunt to stunt, giving the audience almost no time to applaud as she achieved one spectacular feat and began another. As I watched, I knew I could never reach her skill, but promised myself to work hard at improving.

The rest of the Buffalo Bill Wild West show proved to be just as exciting. I became so engrossed in the show I didn't notice the man move to Daddy's other side and whisper in his ear.

"Rose, we need to leave, now," Daddy asserted, urgently pulling me up and leading me toward the exit.

"Daddy, what's wrong?"

"Later, just walk quickly and stay by my side."

Several minutes later we had left the arena. That's when three other men joined the man who had spoken to Daddy and remained like guards, surrounding and guiding us from the area. I noticed three carriages waiting at the entrance gate, and more men seemed to be controlling the crowd and making way for us. Only then did I realized something bad must have happened.

Once we were seated in the second carriage, and it had begun to move, Daddy spoke. "Rose, the Harrisons and Jacksons have disappeared from the ranch. These men are with the STTIU and will escort us back to our time and explain what they know."

BUFFALO BILL'S WILD WEST·
CONGRESS, ROUGH RIDERS OF THE WORLD.

MISS ANNIE OAKLEY,
THE PEERLESS LADY WING-SHOT.

5
Nellie's Book Award

Greg here again. Rose left on the 7th of June, and we expected her to return about the 16th with her father. After Dad and I rode back in from our short reconnaissance trip, I remained grounded and bored.

I think the letter arrived for Nellie on the 10th of June, stating she'd won an award for her latest historical romance book. I guess the award was some kind of a big deal, because she received phone calls from reporters and spent the day sending out press releases. A story about her even appeared on the local news the next evening. On the 12th, a book agent arrived at the ranch and talked with Nellie for several hours. After the agent left, Nellie and Mom conversed for an hour or more over coffee and finally decided Nellie should meet with the agent again in Kansas City and perhaps speak with an attorney she knew there about the possible publishing deal. I guessed our Nellie was going to become a famous, big name author. Anyway, all those events led to Mom, Dad, Nellie, and James deciding to fly to Kansas City for a brief stay.

Later that day, Dad received a warning from the Pirate in the mail. Can you believe he actually mailed it? I'm not sure what it said, as Dad would not share it with me, but the results were that I would get to go along on the trip. No one trusted me to be left home alone, especially with the Pirate still on the loose.

After Dad made all the arrangements, he called the STTIU and updated our location status for the following week. Something all adult TTIs had to do, especially those who worked for the Investigative Unit.

"What a strange call. The connection was horrible, lots of static and background noise," Dad reported to James at dinner on the evening of the 13th.

"Did the agent have an explanation?" James asked.

"Said something I couldn't quite catch about sending an email instead, as their phones were not working properly. I went ahead and sent in our status change by email, but even with our secure server, I hated having to do so."

"I doubt anyone cares about our travel plans enough to read our emails, Ken," stated Mom. "What time do you want to leave again? I need to let my site supervisor know so he can release Melissa to come over and stay here while we're away."

"I want to be in the air by 7:00 a.m., and Greg, make sure you walk Boone and put him in his crate well before our departure time."

"Come on Dad, let me take him with us?" I pleaded.

"Not this time. I couldn't find a pet friendly hotel. Besides, he'll be happier here where he can run and look after the place. Your mother has already arranged for one of her technicians to come and take care of Boone and the horses."

"Don't worry, Greg, Melissa will arrive about 6:00 a.m. to begin laboratory and computer analysis. You know her, and she knows Boone. He'll be fine," Mom stated.

Knowing when *not* to continue my pleading, I instead turned the conversation to our trip. "So what are we going to do while Nellie and James meet with the agent and lawyer?"

"Oh, we have some side trips planned. Now, finish your supper and get packed."

Packed? I crammed clean underwear, a clean pair of jeans, a somewhat clean pair of shorts, and three shirts in a duffel. I packed my tablet. Hotels give you toothbrushes. Right?

At 5:30 a.m., Dad knocked on my door and made sure I was awake. I hate getting up early, unless *I* want to, but at least with this trip I would not be bored out of my mind as I had been most of the spring. Like usual, Nellie had packed her normal *breakfast-to-go* for each of us. I walked Boone and placed him in his crate right before joining Dad for the preflight check. I had been secretly planning to ask for flying lessons next Christmas, so I wanted Dad to see me taking an interest in all that goes into flying a small plane. Once Dad took off, we all breakfasted in the air. Nellie had outdone herself. We each had biscuits with Canadian bacon and this thick maple blackberry jam combination. It was heaven. I ate two, then I took a nap, so I missed the urgent in-flight call Dad received right as we approached Nebraska air space. I awoke just as the plane touched down on a rural airport, not much more than the landing strip we had at the ranch.

As we taxied to a stop, I noticed a tall man and a slim woman, both dressed in suits, next to a large SUV parked near the end of the taxiway.

"James, do you know those two agents?" Dad asked.

"Never seen either one before. They must be out of one of the western stations," James replied.

"Guess we better see what's up, and why we were diverted here."

Taxiing to a full stop, Dad and James jumped from the plane and jogged toward the waiting car, while Mom and Nellie began discussing how this detour might make us late for her meetings. Their talk ended rather suddenly when the tall man pulled a gun and shot out one of the plane's front tires. Dad and James had nowhere to hide or run, so they both fell to the tarmac. Mom screamed, and Nellie pushed her toward the floor. Then the woman in the suit raised a bullhorn-type speaker.

"Emily, Nellie, and Greg, get out of the plane and lie down on the tarmac. Do it now, and no one will get hurt."

Thinking quickly, I pulled my cell phone from my pocket, and noticing I had no coverage, used the note taking function to record a message. As I prepared to jump from the plane, I stuffed my phone down between the seat cushion and back of the copilot's seat.

We had no choice. The tall man had an automatic rifle pointed right at Dad and James. Things began to happen. Once we left the plane and lay on the ground, the woman approached us with a gun of her own and took Mom and Nellie inside a small hangar. Mom told me later about how the woman had a police-type audio device so she and the man could communicate. Inside the hangar, the woman had directed Mom and Nellie to remove all of their clothing and dress in the nineteenth-century clothing provided for them. The woman threatened to shoot me if they resisted in any way. Nellie said she was humiliated to be treated thus. Mom said she simply grew madder with each passing minute.

Outside, Dad, James, and I had no idea what was happening. But one thing we did know, the man with the gun was the Pirate, and he was in control.

"If any of you move, I'll shoot you all. I don't want to harm you. I generally don't believe in violence, but Ken, you and James have made my life a living hell. Why do you care if I steal from history?" the Pirate asked vehemently.

Dad started to answer, only to be told to shut up and lie still. I guess the Pirate's question was a rhetorical one.

"Take out your cell phones and place them in front of you on the ground," he ordered. Dad and James hesitated and then did as he directed.

I pretended to search frantically through my pockets for my phone and then stated loudly, "Darn, I left my phone at the ranch."

I don't think the Pirate believed me, and both Dad and James gave me strange looks.

After they changed clothes, the gun-toting woman ushered Mom and Nellie back outside to join us, and she took over guard duty. The Pirate took James and me inside the hangar and made us strip and change into rustic mid-nineteenth century clothing. We each had canvas trousers with suspenders, a cotton shirt, wool vest, leather boots, and boiled wool slouch hats. I refuse to describe our underwear, if you can call it that. I tried to leave on my woven bracelet with the coin hidden inside, but he made me remove it. Next, he marched us back outside, told us to lie down beside Mom and Nellie, and took Dad inside to change. I half-expected Dad to pull some fancy move and take the Pirate out, but nope, he just went along and did as he was told. I'd already figured out we were going to be forced to jump to some time in the 1800s and left there. Why else would they have made sure we had no items from the present when we jumped? Only when touching an artifact dating from some year in the past can TTIs time-jump. To return to their own time, they need an artifact created in that year.

Only when Dad returned did I really get worried. Not so much for us, as for Dad. He hated being told to do something he didn't want to do and had always been protective of Mom and me.

The Pirate spoke quietly this time. "I am going to hand you one coin, only one. All of you are to place a finger on the coin and jump at once. If any of you stay behind, I will shoot you. I have provided you with transportation, supplies, and food. You'll have a choice to make; go West or return east. However, if you return east, I will be waiting for you, and I'll kill you all. I am giving you your lives. Not *in this time*, but at least you will have a chance to create a good life for yourself. Now, get to your feet."

James and I rose and helped Mom and Nellie get to their feet. Getting up in those long skirts and petticoats was difficult enough, but even harder when you're shaking with fear and anger. I could tell Mom wanted to attack both the Pirate and his companion. Nellie just seemed to be stunned. Dad hopped up and stood glaring at the Pirate. Once we were all standing, the Pirate flipped Dad a coin. I saw him sneak a peek at the date.

"Now, get in a circle, and all of you touch that coin," the Pirate's companion directed.

As we all reached out to touch it, I could see in Dad's eyes that he was planning something. Realizing he would be sacrificing himself for us, I figured I'd better take over and make this jump happen. Dad extended the coin toward James, while looking him in the eyes and winking. He whispered, "Go. I'll handle this." Just as the rest of us reached for the coin, I realized I couldn't let Dad take the chance. Even if it meant living out my life in another time, I couldn't let him be hurt, so as I touched the coin, I grabbed his arm and took us all to 1853.

6
Covered Wagons

At first, Dad frowned at me. After about half a minute, he smiled, "Looks like *you* decided we're better off here together, Greg. Oh, well, let's see where we stand."

"Ken," Mom gasped. "What are we going to do?"

"Looks to me, Emily, like we're going west," Dad replied, pointing to two covered wagons, often called Prairie Schooners. They stood where the airplane hangar had been, beside a buckboard, horses, eight oxen, and several light brown dairy cows. Each of the wagons stood mired in dried mud. I realized they had been there for several days, or even weeks.

Instead of an airport tarmac, we now stood on an open prairie. I could see a river a short distance away, but nothing else. No buildings, no people, nothing. I looked up and saw only birds. No airplanes. Yep, 1853.

While James spoke with Nellie, I took Mom's hand and pulled her into a hug. "It'll be okay," I whispered. "Dad's with us. We can handle anything." Of course, I felt more worried than I let on, but if there is anything I've learned from my previous time travel adventures, it's that panic gets you nowhere. Better to go with the flow.

We spent the better part of the morning discussing/arguing about our options, such as a possible rescue by the STTIU after they realized we were missing. We moved on to the dangers we faced, and at last, began making an inventory of our supplies. Not that the discussion stopped. We continued to discuss *a possible rescue* for the next few days.

Seemed the Pirate meant what he said. He'd provided us with transportation, food, and supplies. Both covered wagons stood ready to be hitched to the oxen—four for each wagon. I knew the pioneers often used oxen because they were stronger than horses and able to pull large loads. Also, an ox will eat native grasses, whereas a horse often needed additional food, such as grains, to remain healthy. Oxen are nothing more than neutered male cows, making them more manageable and less temperamental. Besides the oxen, we had five horses, three dairy cows, and one calf. The buckboard, a small flat wagon, could be pulled by one of the horses. Like the wagons, a canvas, stretched tight across its bed, covered a number of mysterious lumps. Which horse would pull the buckboard was easy to figure out. Ever seen those commercials with the draft horses pulling the beer wagon? Well, one of our horses looked a lot like a Clydesdale—huge muscular body with those big dinner plate-sized hooves. Mom said ours was a Percheron, a French breed. He was a big dappled gray stallion, with a white mane and tail.

Mom and Nellie took over inventorying the goods inside the two wagons. Each wagon contained well-organized boxes of foodstuffs, including flour, cornmeal, sugar, coffee, tea, salt bacon, and lard, along with two additional sets of clothing for each of us. Some of the clothing hung along the inside of the canvases. Nellie's initial search found blankets and quilts, pillows, India rubber waterproof mats, tin utensils and plates, and cast iron pots and pans, including a Dutch oven. Soon Mom and Nellie decided everything would need to be removed, inventoried, and returned to the wagons so we would know exactly what we had and didn't have. Mom and Nellie commenced creating a plan of action of how to go about this monumental task.

"Emily, we can't do that. We'll just have to find out what we have as we go along," Dad admonished sharply.

"Ken Harrison, if you think I will start a trip of this length and magnitude without knowing what we might need to buy, IF we find a place to purchase additional items, you are badly mistaken. Oh, did that blasted Pirate even leave us with any money?" Mom demanded.

"No need to worry," shouted James, "look what I found."

I turned to see him scrambling from the back of the second wagon holding two books and several sheets of paper.

"Look! John C. Fremont's *The Report of the Exploring Expedition to the Rocky Mountains in the year 1842, and to Oregon and North California in the Years 1843-44* and Palmer's *Journal of Travels over the Rocky Mountains to the Mouth of the Columbia River made during the years 1845 and 1846 containing minute descriptions of the valleys of the Willamette, Umpqua, and Clamet, etc. . .* He also left a complete inventory and this," James finished, tossing a leather pouch to Dad.

My recent home school unit on the Westward Expansion mentioned these two books as the ones some wagon trains carried as guide books. The two books mapped out the various trails and provided settlers with a guide to the various Indian tribes, river crossings, wildlife, and plants along the routes, both to Oregon and California.

While James and Dad counted the money in the pouch, most of it in gold coins, Nellie and Mom studied the inventory list. The Pirate had been quite generous, both with the gold and our supplies. Neatly packed, we had: 125 lbs. of flour for each of us, 150 lbs. of sugar, 100 lbs. of coffee, 50 lbs. of tea, and 200 lbs. of cornmeal along with 300 lbs. of lard, 600 lbs. of bacon, and some sour pickles, the last three packed in small barrels. Heavy cloth sacks contained dried beans, rice, dried fruit, and various spices including salt and pepper. We found bottles of vinegar, molasses, sorghum, honey, and baking soda, and eggs packed in the cornmeal. Cheese packed in cloth and hardtack crackers were stored in a wooden box. We also had two wooden crates with three hens in each hanging on the sides of the wagons. I guessed right off these would be for eggs, not for eating. We didn't have a rooster. Hanging from each wagon was a bucket where milk from the cows would be churned into butter as we traveled each day, simply by the action of the swinging bucket. We also had two butter churns. I hoped I never had to use one. It's hard work, as I knew from a previous journey into the past.

The written inventory also listed four rifles and three pistols with saddle holsters. Dad, James, and I found the guns in a wooden box attached to the outside of one wagon. Someone had wrapped each in oil cloth. We found ammunition packed in the bottom of the crate. We carefully examined each firearm. There were two Hawken rifles. I knew the so-called mountain men and early settlers commonly used these .50 caliber, muzzle-loading rifles on the prairies and in the Rocky Mountains. We also had two breech-loading Sharps rifles. They fired .52

caliber rounds and weighed about 9.5 pounds each, somewhat less than the heavy 15-pound Hawken. For pistols, we had three Colt Third Model Dragoons. Dad owned a reproduction Third Model that I had fired several times. It has a folding leaf sight, fires a .44 caliber ball, and is effective to about 80 yards.

James picked up a pistol he found in the bottom of the box and stared at it, turning it over and over in his hands. "Ken, look, a Walter Colt. I wonder where the Pirate stole this from."

"Why do you think he stole it?" I asked.

"Greg, these pistols are rare. Even during their time of manufacture, they were rare. Colt only made about 1,100 of them. A few years ago, one sold for almost a million dollars," he replied. "I doubt the Pirate just went out and bought one for our use."

"It's not on the inventory, and neither is this 12-gauge Greener shotgun," Dad interjected. "I wonder what else might not be on that inventory. Looks like someone without the Pirate's knowledge of valuable historical artifacts placed some of the items in the wagon. Perhaps his accomplice?"

Other necessities on the list included four saddles, none of them side saddles, which made Mom happy, since she refuses to ride side saddle. There were hunting knives, cooking knives, buckets, and even a folding sheet iron stove attached to the back of one wagon. At the side of each wagon were India rubber water cans that held about five gallons each. They had already been filled. Nellie pointed out how the medical kit contained only medicines of the time, like physic pills, essence of peppermint, and caster oil, with none of our modern antibiotics. There were also books. I found copies of the *Bible*, *Uncle Tom's Cabin*, *The House of the Seven Gables*, *The Collected Works of Edgar Allen Poe*, and Elizabeth Barrett Browning's *Sonnets from the Portuguese*. There were a few others, each one wrapped in oilcloth. So much for me finishing *In the Heart of a Mustang* by M.J. Evans. I figured, I'd just have to learn to like Poe.

The wagons also held furniture like chairs, tables, and even a bedstead in one. Both contained a feather tick mattress. Dad showed me how some of the extra boards in the wagons could be used to make a bed by placing them across the boxes on each side and putting the feather tick on top. Mom found candles, lanterns and lantern oil, although not very much. None of these were on the inventory list.

Checking out the buckboard, I discovered some of the foodstuff barrels were packed in the wagon's bed, and covered with a heavy canvas, that smelled of something I couldn't quite identify. I asked Dad about it, and he told me the canvas for the wagons and the buckboard would have been soaked in linseed oil to make them water repellent. *Repellent*, meaning they could get wet and leak, but would repel water to a certain extent. The buckboard also contained farming implements, seeds, other tools like shovels and axes, mixed grain and corn for the livestock, and various wagon parts. In the wagons, Nellie discovered more clothing for cold weather, rain slickers, hats and bonnets, and even heavy leather gloves. Someone had even been gracious enough to include several yards of both calico and wool, along with a sewing kit.

The afternoon came and then passed. We still hadn't moved an inch. I noticed Dad and Mom talking, then Dad and James, then James and Nellie, then all four together. Finally, Dad called me over.

"Greg, we've all discussed our options. Now that I think about it, we should've asked your opinion, being as you're fourteen and should have a say in what we do."

I started to interrupt, but Dad held up his hand to stop me.

"Son, looks like we have two options. Go back to St. Louis or somewhere else in the East and take our chances with the Pirate and his partner, or partners, or go west. We can decide along the way, whether it will be California or Oregon. Most of us feel going west is the best option. We don't know how many accomplices he has, but he would have an advantage if we traveled back to any city or town. He is most likely having us watched and without knowing who all of our enemies are, I think we are safer if we go west. Besides, in 1853, James and Nellie would need papers proving they are free if we turn east. In the west, they could probably survive without them. California is a free state, and Oregon is a free territory."

"Dad, I just finished a unit on the wagon trains, and we're more than a month behind schedule. None of the trains started out this late; most settlers left in late April or early May to get over the mountains before the snows began."

"James and I discussed this. I think if we push hard for the next month, we might catch up with some of the later travelers. We're well supplied, the river crossings should be low, and we have fresh oxen. We're not at the starting point most trains used, but are already about 100 miles west along the trail."

This time Mom interrupted, "Ken, do you know where we are? Can you find the Oregon Trail?"

"Yeah . . . well, we're west of the Missouri River, somewhere north of the main trail, on the Big Blue River. I think we can turn southwest after crossing this river and find the Little Blue River. Or we can go almost due west, and that will lead us to the Platte River and then to Fort Kearney. It should be about 65 miles to the Little Blue or the Platte, maybe three days journey. Right now, I suggest we learn how to hitch oxen to a wagon. And since none of us have eaten much since breakfast, perhaps we should make a campfire and dinner? Greg, how about you gather up some firewood?"

And so, our first night on the trail began. Firewood proved hard to find, and so I saddled a horse, planning to search along the river bank. Immediately, Mom and Nellie started worrying about me getting lost until Dad put his foot down, so to speak.

"Emily, stop, just stop. He survived in prehistoric times and wandered all over central Kentucky during an Indian war. You let him and Rose ride alone in North Dakota. I think he can follow a river and find firewood."

Mom relented and began helping Nellie.

The sun had fallen almost below the horizon by the time we supped on Nellie's biscuits, bacon, and eggs, while sitting on blankets about a campfire. Nellie pulled a folding chair from one wagon and busied herself preparing beans to soak overnight. Dad and James loaded the rifles and pistols. We made sure the livestock had not wandered too far. The horses were hobbled, but the oxen and cows just grazed where they wished. Coyotes howled in the distance, but that was one sound we found familiar. I pulled one of the waterproof mats and some blankets from a wagon and bedded down underneath it for the night. I heard Dad and Mom rearrange some things to fold out the bed platform in the wagon and top it with the feather tick. I guess Nellie and James did the same in the other wagon.

It took a long time to fall asleep. I wondered about what would become of us. I worried about the dangers of this trip. And I fretted about Boone. And Rose. Would anyone ever figure out what became of us? I watched stars move across the sky, saw the moon rise, and caught a glimpse of a shooting star. I could hear coyotes and even wolves. I heard small animals rustling in the grass near the horses. They snorted in annoyance. At some point I fell asleep, still cursing the Pirate.

7
On the Trail West

I would have slept later, as was my usual fashion, but Dad, James, and Nellie got up at sunrise. Dad shook me awake soon after.

"Son, help Nellie with the fire, and then come help hitch the oxen."

Okay, so making a fire's easy—wood, kindling, matches. Hitching eight oxen—not so easy. Funny, but not easy. You see, oxen live to eat, to graze on grass, not to pull a 2,500 pound wagon. They may be more docile than bulls, but they're still large, strong creatures, each with a mind of his own. Last night around the fire, Mom and Nellie named the oxen. Big Brown looked just like his name, not a spot of any other color. Speck's hide blended colors from black to gray to white. Lucy and Desi were reddish brown all over, except for a white patch on Lucy's nose. (Yes, they knew it was a male animal – didn't seem to matter to Mom or Nellie.) The other four had speckled brown and white hides, making them hard to tell apart, until you looked at their ears. Lefty sported a white left ear, and Righty just the opposite.

Short Tail, well, isn't the name obvious? And finally, there's Spook. He jumped at any sound and anyone approaching.

After hearing those names, Dad and I named four of the horses. We started with the large, solid black stallion, *Midnight*. The two mares came next. James helped and named the gray one *Ghost*. I named the black and white pinto *Clown*, because she often did funny things like stepping over invisible objects and walking sideways. Last came a bay gelding. His name caused quite a bit of discussion. He had no distinguishing markings, was calm, and grazed peacefully among our little herd. We tried several names, but none of them seemed to fit until we turned to find him eating a biscuit Nellie had accidentally left in the large cast-iron Dutch oven. So, he earned the moniker *Biscuit*.

Each of our oxen has a ring in their nose. To guide them into the traces, you simply grab their nose ring and lead them where you want them to go. So Dad and James each grabbed an ox and headed toward the river. The others, except for Spook, followed. He walked in the other direction in a leisurely manner, indicating he wasn't thirsty. As the other seven drank their fill, James went back for Spook. James tried slipping up on him, calling to him quietly, shooing him toward the river, and something Nellie called "dances with ox" after that movie "Dances with Wolves." None of this had much effect on Spook except he moved farther and farther away from our camp and the river. Meanwhile, Dad grabbed Big Brown's nose ring and led him to our wagon. Speck, Lucy, and Desi followed along like puppies. Impressive.

Once near our wagon, Dad slipped a neck bow over each ox. Then he picked up one of the large wooden yokes and placed it across Big Brown's and Speck's shoulders while they were standing side by side. Then he removed their neck bows, placed them under their necks, pushed the ends of each up through holes in the yoke, and pinned each neck bow in place. I noticed he would examine each yoke once in place and changed them around a bit between the various oxen. Dad explained how each pair of oxen had a particular yoke that fitted them better. This kept the yoke from rubbing and making sores.

"Dad, how did you learn to do this?"

"Oh, I watched a YouTube video made at an historic park demonstration," he replied without even cracking a smile.

Right.

Dad placed Desi and Lucy side by side and yoked them together. He moved them behind Big Brown and Speck. Dad told the oxen to back up, over and over again, while snapping a short whip attached to a short rod. He never actually hit them. When they had backed into place over the falling tongue of the wagon, he set the double tree and its attached single trees into place. All of this connected to the wagon's front axle. At last, Dad connected all the ropes and chains, and our wagon stood ready to roll.

James still wandered, and sometimes ran about, trying to catch Spook. All three of the remaining oxen moved over the tongue of the other wagon and waited to be hitched. I stepped over to try my hand at it, while Dad went to help James. As Spook moved away, James tried roping him. Now James is good at a lot of things around a ranch, but we all noticed that roping was not something he had any talent or skill at doing. About this time, Mom came up from the riverbank where she had been refilling the water containers.

"James, what *are* you doing?" she called. Then, after watching James and Dad try to catch Spook, she calmly walked out and approached Spook from the front, all the while humming softly. She walked right up to him, grabbed his nose ring, and led him to the front yoke of the Jackson's wagon. I think she hummed the theme to "Ghost Busters." We had him harnessed in no time, and he behaved like a well-trained domestic animal as long as you hummed to him. Strange.

James rounded up the horses and saddled Midnight. I hitched Budweiser to the buckboard. Yep, we named the draft horse *Budweiser*.

Now, none of us, not one, except for Dad, had ever driven a wagon pulled by oxen. Dad really didn't learn how to hitch them from a YouTube video. He obviously had some experience, but didn't take the time to tell that story, as we were anxious to be on our way. First, he gave Mom and Nellie lessons while James and I consumed biscuits and bacon and drank coffee.

Mom proved to be a quick learner. Nellie, who, until earlier this year, had avoided horses and all large animals, refused.

"I will not put this venture at risk by driving a wagon. I'm sure I'll tip the whole thing over before we reach the first river crossing. No, I'm not doing it. I'll walk."

"Nellie," Mom pleaded, "we have three wagons, that means three drivers. Someone has to scout ahead and hunt for game. There are only five of us."

"You **will not** change my mind," she stated and walked off toward the west.

Dad shrugged and then gave James a quick lesson. James seemed hesitant at first, but willing. Mom and I doused the fire, placed all the cooking utensils back in the wagons, and mounted up. Dad rode Midnight. James and Mom drove wagons, and I drove the buckboard. We tied the other horses, one behind each covered wagon and the buckboard. After some rounding up by Dad, the cows followed us as we moved out of camp.

As a group, we'd decided to try and cover twenty-five to thirty miles each of the first few days. Most wagon trains traveled only about twelve to twenty miles a day, so our plan was ambitious.

Mom took the lead because Big Brown did. James followed, and I pulled up the rear of our little train. Sometimes we drove in single file and often side by side. We caught up with Nellie about a mile away. I persuaded her to ride beside me on and off for the rest of the day, but she covered a lot of the twenty-five miles we traveled that day on foot. Mom and James could drive the wagons from the seats; however, ox teams work just as well if the driver walks beside the lead ox and guides him with a whip. I noticed Mom and James both used this method, so each ended up walking for most of the day.

Our first obstacle came early in the morning. Dad rode off and returned some fifteen minutes later to tell us of a good ford for crossing the Big Blue. We turned alongside the tree-covered bank and rode due west for about a mile before we came to a low ford. Mom looked hesitant about driving the oxen into the water, but Big Brown just took the lead and waded right in. At the crossing, the water stood only about two feet deep, and the bottom was sandy with bits of gravel. We crossed without incident. Nellie rode across with me and then stepped down and returned to walking.

The day passed with a slow repetition of prairie grass, a few small creeks, and one rolling hill after another. I could smell prairie grass and feel light breezes on and off throughout the day. As the day grew warmer and warmer, I removed my wool vest and rolled my sleeves up as far as I could. I longed for one of my t-shirts, which are so much cooler. I did wear the hat most of the day to keep the sun out of my eyes.

I mentioned to Nellie something I had read from my study unit in a pioneer woman's diary. The settler had noted the lack of firewood on the prairie and how she had picked up any wood she saw and carried it along in the wagon. Nellie began doing this, and we even stopped by a few creeks to load up what we found along the banks. It was easy to catch up with the wagons, as Budweiser could move along more quickly than the oxen.

Lunch consisted of more biscuits and bacon, leftovers from breakfast. We drank lots of water, using a common dipper from one of the wagon's barrels. The sun shone bright all day, but a wind blew constantly, keeping us cooler as we bounced along. Bounced, bumped, rattled, whatever you call it. By noon, my bum ached from repeatedly hitting the solid wood seat on the buckboard. I noticed Mom massaging her backside as she climbed down after one of the stream crossings. I'd never realized how rough prairie ground can be.

Dad scouted ahead for several miles, and then would ride back and tell us to veer one way or another to find good stream crossings, or just to avoid obstacles. By midday, my hands had blisters from handling the reins. Budweiser would ramble along for a while without any guidance from me, and then I would need to turn to avoid a rock or rough stream crossing. We were not yet on any westward trail, just crossing the wide-open prairie.

The scenery changed not at all—all day prairie grass, hills, and streams. We saw one person on horseback in the distance. Dad told us later it was a Pawnee man. We saw no game other than a few rabbits. Dad shot three during the day and brought them back already cleaned and ready to be cooked for dinner. At lunch, he switched horses and rode Clown for the rest of the day.

I'd thought I would die of boredom back at our ranch when I was grounded. No, this was boredom! At least at home, I could read or play a video game or even do school work. I soon discovered that driving a wagon hour after hour after hour is worse. Once, I even fell asleep. At least when Nellie rode with me I had someone to talk to and you know how I love to talk. I think that's why Nellie often got down and walked.

Boredom ended at night fall. Dad told us to pull the wagons in close at a small stream running from a clear cold spring. We filled our water containers before watering the stock. James and I hobbled the horses and picketed each with ropes and stakes, allowing them to wander some and graze. The oxen and cattle we left to their own devices, just keeping watch so they didn't wander too far.

The firewood we had collected came in handy, and Nellie produced beans with molasses and bacon, corn muffins with butter, and coffee with cream and sugar. Mom roasted the rabbits on a spit over the campfire. We ate as though starved, and little remained after five hungry pioneers had finished. While our meal cooked, James read to us from Fremont's guide book. The first chapters covered the area east of where we began our trip. Fremont's party had encountered several Indians from the Pawnee and Otoe tribes. The explorers had found plenty of game, but that was 1843. Since then, ten years of travelers rolling across the area had reduced the number of deer, elk, and antelope in the area. The large herds of bison now avoided this portion of the prairie, staying much to the north.

The moon hung large in the sky when, dead tired, all of us took to our beds and settled in. If the coyotes and wolves came near, I never heard them.

8

A Hungry American Indian

Mom and Nellie decided to drive the buckboard the next day, so I had to drive our wagon. James and Dad harnessed the oxen, and I helped the ladies put Budweiser in his traces. We all had hot coffee, but everything else for the morning meal was cold, as Dad wanted an early start. The day began hot, and the heat grew with every hour. The terrain changed little, only becoming more sandy. We passed some almost dry creek beds, a bad omen for later in the summer.

I took the time while driving to examine our wagon. Mom and Dad had rolled up the heavy hemp canvas on both sides to give the inside some ventilation. They had tied the canvas to the hickory bows that gave our wagon its familiar shape and made it look like sails on a boat. The wide back wheels stood almost six feet high, while the front wheels seemed to be only about four feet in diameter. This allowed them to turn without hitting the sides of the wagon. I had noticed the axles were massive, which probably kept them from breaking. We carried a spare in the buckboard. Hanging from the rear axle was a bucket containing grease for the wheels' hubs. In the rear, a brake lever could be used to keep the wagon from rolling when stopped. This lever worked the brakes attached to the rear wheels.

A platform just inside the front of the wagon served as a seat, and I could place my feet on the jockey box attached to the front outside of the wagon. It held the necessary tools to make repairs to wagons or harnesses. Inside the wagon, everything looked jumbled and crowded, but actually the items were placed just so and secured for travel. Straps, hooks, and pegs provided ways to secure clothing, tarps, bedclothes, ropes, etc..., so nothing moved or shifted during rough travel.

Just before we started out, Dad did something to a gadget on one of the rear wheels on the other wagon.

"Hey, Dad, what's in the leather case?"

"Come see. I discovered it last night. It's called a Roadometer. This paper says it will record wheel revolutions by the mile and quarter mile, so we can figure out the distances we travel each day. It's ingenious! I'd never heard of this invention before. It says Jas. (that's an abbreviation for James) Green of Baltimore made it. You set the measurement based on the wheel size. Since we have six foot wheels, 880 rotations mark a mile. We must reset it each day."

"Wicked! Do both wagons have one?"

"Nope, only this one on James' wagon. I'll tell him about it later."

The day dragged on and on. I walked most of the way, wishing I had better boots or even my sneakers. Our oxen behaved well, crossed the mostly dry streams without even slowing, and managed to splash me with water at each wet crossing. At least I was cooler until the sun dried out my clothes.

Mom and Nellie took turns driving the buckboard and walking. Nellie had conceded to learn how to drive after a long talk with James and Mom. I noticed Nellie also had Mom picking up any firewood they saw along the way. The top of the buckboard's canvas soon looked as though someone had chopped down a tree, removed all its limbs, and loaded them for hauling off. Like the day before, we lunched on leftovers. Although it was only day two, I was growing tired of bacon and biscuits and jerky. I felt desperate to return to my time. Was anyone looking for us? Did Rose even know we were missing?

The day's heat rolled up into a storm late in the day. We noticed the clouds and then the whirling sand that soon caused us to tie our kerchiefs around our faces. The wind rose to a howl just before the rain came in one straight downpour. No warning, just rain. Then it stopped. That's when James called out for us to take shelter under the wagons. With no time to unhitch, we set the brakes on each wagon and watched the massive storm blow across the prairie. Then came the hail, about golf-ball sized. It stung when it hit. Our cows scattered, and Dad pelted after them on horseback. James and I calmed our remaining horses. Our oxen still in their traces, nervously moved about during the hail storm.

After the storm abated, Mom and Nellie made what they called an executive decision, and sent me ahead on Clown to find water and a place to camp. I soon returned, having discovered a small creek about one quarter mile distant. While we established a camp, Nellie began making our evening meal. She soon had rabbits roasting on a spit and beans cooking in a big Dutch oven. I saw her mix up corn bread and peel apples, for what I hoped would be her famous apple pan dowdy.

"Nellie, how much longer? I'm starving," I asked after changing into dry clothes and hanging my wet ones on a line stretched between the two wagons.

"Young man, this can't be rushed. The fire needs to be hot. I have no stove, no oven; besides, you're always hungry. Now go fetch my stool and help your mother with the horses," Nellie replied sharply.

I found Mom hobbling the horses. It took her a while to place the woven leather straps around each horse's front legs to keep them from wandering too far. James had taken the oxen to water, and we could see Dad in the far distance, returning with the cows. The quiet of the evening settled around us as we each concentrated on our chores and made camp, yet again.

That's when we heard the long, high-pitched scream.

James, Mom, and I dropped what we were doing and rushed back to camp to find Nellie standing, stunned, still holding her iron skillet and spatula, while a young American Indian boy stood pointing and screaming. I couldn't decide who looked more scared. The boy stared at Nellie, pointing and shaking, but kept a good distance away. He kept glancing at the rabbits on the spit, but circled Nellie, pointing and jabbering in his native language. When James arrived, running into camp last, the boy fell to the ground and pointed at him instead of Nellie.

"Nellie, James, relax," Mom urged. "I think he's hungry and scared. Also, I don't think he's ever seen a black person before."

Nellie lowered her skillet and settled casually on the ground near the fire. She placed the skillet to the side and reached over to grab a leftover biscuit. She held it out to the boy. He continued to stare and point, but at last he stopped screaming and jabbering. None of us moved for what seemed like hours. I heard Dad ride into camp and tie his horse. He stood just where he was. Finally, I guess hunger overcame fear, as the boy reached for the biscuit and scarfed it down in two bites. Nellie held out her arm and smoothed her hand up and down. Then, she held it up showing how her color had not rubbed off. After doing this twice, she motioned to James and he repeated the movement. The boy watched, mesmerized by the sight, but seemed to come to an understanding. Soon he sat at the edge of the fire and turned the spit, making sure the rabbits cooked evenly. Nellie watched his every move, and he hers. His eyes left her only to check on the rabbits.

Dad approached and pulled Mom and James aside. The three of them conferred for several minutes before Dad spoke, "Nellie, Greg, I think his family is gone. I passed a burned-out village while chasing the cows. Looks like it happened recently. There are several burned bodies scattered here and there. I don't know if we'll ever know the full story, but for now, it looks like we might have a passenger. Be friendly but wary. I don't want him trying to steal a horse."

"Ken, should we go back and bury the bodies?" James asked.

"I think we'd better leave them to the scavengers. I know it's cruel, but I think the best we can do is care for this survivor."

We found out just how starved the boy was when Nellie placed the food on our tin plates. He ate the beans with his hands and cleaned the rabbit bones of any speck of meat until they looked white. At last, he used cornbread to scrape the last remaining bits from his plate. Only when Nellie spooned out the apple pan dowdy did he hesitate. Nellie served it from the pan onto our plates, and I could see the steam rising in the cooling evening air. The boy stared as I took a spoonful and began blowing on it until it cooled some. He finally poked his with a finger and licked off the luscious juice the apples and sugars had created. Then, he pointed at my spoon. I found one and passed it to him, then showed him how to hold it and scoop up the dessert.

Now, I'm a fast eater, but our guest finished his portion long before any of us. Nellie reached to give him a bit more, but he held out his hand and placed his plate on the ground near the fire. As he rose, we realized he meant to leave. We had come to where our mutual lack of language created a real dilemma. Using a lot of gestures, we urged him to stay, and he returned to sit by the fire. He watched in awe as Mom and Nellie washed the dishes, put away the remaining food, and made things ready for bed.

"Emily, do you think he'll stay?" Dad asked.

"I don't know. He's a child still. I'd guess only about five or six years old. I think he fears being alone, but is also still scared of us, especially Nellie and James. How about we give him a blanket and show him where we sleep? I think he might stay, at least for the night. I couldn't rest easy if he were out on the prairie alone."

He stayed. He curled up with a blanket about three feet from where I lay under Mom and Dad's wagon. I tried to get him to move onto the waterproof mat with me, but Mom suggested he might have lice, so I didn't try too hard. I watched as he fell asleep and heard him whimper when dreams invaded his slumber. He remained asleep after most of us had risen the next morning. After a while, I touched his arm, and he rose, glancing about in fear.

I motioned for him to follow me to the stream, where we could wash up for the day. I had discovered a deeper pool about one hundred yards upstream and stripped down to take a quick bath. As I jumped into the water, the boy realized what I intended and pulled off the ratty doeskin shirt that seemed to be all he wore except for his beaded mocassins. I dove underwater and only surfaced once he joined me in the cool stream.

When James and Dad appeared a moment or two later, I managed to speak while they stripped. "Hey, I think you ought to know—HE'S a GIRL."

Mom and Nellie proved just as surprised when we returned to camp with the news of our discovery. They tried to bundle her up in one of my shirts and she gave in, but when Nellie produced a comb and tried to remove the tangles from her hair, we discovered she could scream and run. James caught her and calmed her down. We watched as they sat under a tree on the river bank. He held her tight and sang some song I didn't know. Mom later told me it's called "Would You Like to Swing on a Star" and how Bing Crosby made it famous during World War II. I *had* heard of Bing Crosby. James has a fine baritone voice, and soon the girl sat mesmerized in his lap, stroking his short curly beard and smiling.

She rode or walked beside James all day, leaving his side only to tend to nature's call and to help Nellie and Mom gather firewood. Our third day started late and ended late. We'd established somewhat of a routine by then. Everyone had their chores. We would make camp while Nellie started cooking. The rest of us looked after the animals. Mom did most of the milking. James tended the oxen, and Dad and I took care of the horses, carried water, and hunted for game when necessary.

Over dinner that evening, Nellie decided the girl needed a name. This created a serious discussion. First Nellie tried. She pointed to herself and said, "Nellie." Then she pointed to James and said, "James." As she proceeded around the campfire speaking each of our names, the girl's eyes followed her every move. Then Nellie pointed to her, thinking she might get the idea. Didn't work. She instead pointed to James and said very clearly, "James." So Nellie began again. Still, no luck. After the fourth or fifth time, Nellie sighed and gave up.

Mom, Dad, and I tried some of the Indian languages we had learned during our time travels. Again, no luck.

At last, Mom gave up and decided to just give her a name and to call her by it, in hopes she would learn to respond. Just as we each started suggesting names, the girl moved to James' lap and said, "James," pointing to him, and "Baidepe," pointing to herself. She pronounced it, with a long "a," in three syllables, something like bay-dep-e. She did this several times before moving her fingers to James' lips. We soon realized she wanted him to sing. He tried a different song, but she folded her arms and frowned until he sang Bing's famous hit.

Even I couldn't help but notice how she, like children of our own time, nestled into his broad arms, her head against his shoulder, and made herself comfortable. Soon she slept. Nellie and James made a pallet for Baidepe in their wagon, and there she slept from that night onward.

9

They Disappeared?

As the men hustled Daddy and me into one of the waiting carriages, I started to ask one of them questions. "What do you mean the Harrisons have disappeared? You didn't mention Greg, has he disappeared too? Are Boone and the horses at the ranch? Why . . .? " Before I could continue, Daddy hushed me.

"Rose, let the man speak."

"Mr. Engram, Rose, here's what we know for sure. Melissa, one of Emily's assistants said they left on the morning of the 14th for Kansas City so Mrs. Jackson could meet with a literary agent and lawyer. Based on what Melissa told us, we did some investigative work and discovered Mrs. Jackson was informed several days earlier that she'd won a major award for one of her books. As I said, the Harrisons, including Greg, and the Jacksons planned to fly to Kansas City. They did not file a change of location report with the STTIU; however, using their plane's secondary transponder, we've located their plane at a small private airfield in Nebraska. The main transponder had been disabled, and the front tire appears to have been shot out."

I started to shake, and Daddy reached his arm around me, right before I took control of myself and stated firmly, "the Pirate."

"Rose, may I call you Rose?" I nodded my head, since he already had once or twice during the last half hour, and replied, "Of course. Now, how can we help?"

"I work with Ken at STTIU, but only James and Ken are assigned to the Pirate case. My name is Samuel Hawthorne. You can call me Sam. I think you might be able to help us figure out what happened. In a few minutes, we will all jump back and then take cars to the airport. From there, a private jet will take us to Dickinson Theodore Roosevelt Regional Airport in Medora. I've arranged for a small plane to take us to the Harrisons' ranch. In the meantime, Rose, I need you to fill me in on the events last spring when the Pirate kidnapped you and Greg. Can you do that? I need details, every detail you can remember."

When we arrived at the airport after time jumping, I noticed someone had packed our belongings from our hotel room, as our suitcases and packages were being brought aboard. Daddy and I entered the Cessna Citation XLS jet and took our seats. Only Sam and one other agent boarded the flight. Sam introduced him as John Bomgarten.

Once we were airborne, John brought us beverages and snacks, seems there was no crew except the pilot and copilot.

We sat in cushioned leather seats facing in a circle toward the middle of the plane. Small tables pulled down on each side from the bulkhead. John set up a digital recorder on one of the small tables, and I told the tale of being kidnapped by the Pirate. Since the agents could also time travel, each man understood how and why Greg and I had done the things we did to escape. Both seemed pretty impressed that we'd spent the night at Theodore Roosevelt's ranch. Sam asked lots of questions. So did Daddy, as he'd never heard the entire story, having been in Africa when it took place. It took almost an hour for me to relay the events to their satisfaction. I decided they needed to know how Greg had spent most of his time since our abduction trying to find out what had happened to the Pirate. I almost forgot to mention how Ken and James had seen the Pirate in San Francisco a day or so before I left for New York. After I threw out that bit of info, Sam and John sauntered to the back of the plane, supposedly to retrieve some sandwiches, and spent a lot of time in quiet conversation.

When they returned to their seats, I finally got a chance to ask questions. "Is Boone at the ranch?"

"Boone?" John replied, looking confused. "Was there another person living at the ranch with the Harrisons?"

"Greg's Australian Shepherd, you know, a dog?"

"Oh, yes, the dog. One of Emily's assistant site managers, Melissa, came to the house to do lab work and to watch over the animals. Boone and the horses are all accounted for," Sam answered.

"What kind of award did Mom Nellie win? I mean, I never even knew she entered one of her books in a contest," I probed.

"We can't determine that. There was a short interview on a local television news program. We found it on their website, but we can't seem to verify her winning an award. Melissa said Emily told her a woman from the contest agency came to the house and spoke with Nellie at length about her prize. It was this woman, whose name we don't know, who suggested Nellie meet with and hire a lawyer. She might even have suggested the lawyer in Kansas City, who actually does exist."

And so the conversation went on and on, with each of us speculating. Our flight to Medora took almost four hours. Then we boarded a small Cessna prop plane and flew to the ranch. When we arrived, we found several other agents had already arrived there. While John and Sam filled them in on our in-flight conversations, I showed Daddy to his room and then escaped to my own room. After dropping my belongings and changing into jeans, a t-shirt, and boots, as I was still dressed in 1880s clothing, I slipped out into the hallway, planning to do my own investigation. First, I sneaked down the hallway, past the kitchen, and into Mom Nellie's office. I knew where she kept her most recent notes. Nothing. No clues. I had hoped she'd left some clues as to their disappearance. I knew Mom Nellie would never just up and leave me—she's, in so many ways, my mom. In succession, I tried Greg's room, Ken's and Emily's offices and bedroom, and James' and Nellie's bedroom. I ended up in the kitchen, looking for Melissa, when I found Daddy.

"Nothing, Daddy, I've tried all their offices and their bedrooms. Not one clue. Obviously, they didn't plan to disappear. The Pirate did this." And I began to cry.

I sobbed on Daddy's shoulder. Then, as my thoughts turned over and over again to the Pirate, I just got MAD. Dangerously MAD. I mean, I hit him over the head with a large rock the last time I saw him, and now I knew I could and would do more if I ever saw him again.

As the evening grew dark, Daddy and I walked to the barn to feed and water the horses. There we found Melissa, taking care of those necessary, everyday chores. Boone sat beside her until we entered the barn, and then, after barking frantically at Daddy, whom he didn't know, he ran and jumped over and over in front of me, begging for attention. As I scratched his ears, Melissa gave us our first clue.

"Rose, Ken and Emily mentioned before they left how they had trouble reaching Ken's office before they departed, something about Ken needing to update their location. Do you know what that means? Could it have anything to do with their disappearance?" she asked.

"Ah, yes. Ken has to report in constantly about his location, in case he's needed. What exactly did he say?"

"Oh, he seemed to think it strange, that when he tried calling, the line had lots of static, and he was instructed to send an email instead. He said he'd done so, but I think he was worried about security on the Internet connection. Does Ken work for some security unit?"

"Rose, leave Melissa to finish this up and let's report this to Sam and John," Daddy urged, leading me from the barn, Boone close on my heels. We left Melissa without answering her question as Ken's job was, well, secret.

At the last minute, Daddy turned and said, "Melissa, can you hang out here for a few more days?"

"Sure, I have plenty of lab and computer work to complete, no problem."

Sam and John met us at the door, and after hearing our news, did a thorough search of Ken's computer. One of the other agents then began to do some specialized technical *stuff* on it I didn't understand. Daddy said he was trying to see if the computer had been tampered with or hijacked. About an hour later, the agent returned to the living room and reported how someone had indeed tampered with the Internet connection and could read and misdirect any communications. It started the day Nellie's visitor came to the ranch.

"I found where Ken had sent the STTIU his change of location. The hijacker rerouted his message. I haven't been able to trace the link back to the person who did it, but I have techs at the office working on it now. One thing is apparent; this whole book award was a set up to lure the Harrisons and Jacksons away from the ranch."

10
Along the Platte River

Dad's ambitious plan to reach Fort Kearny in three days, quickly fell apart. Instead, the fort came into view late in the afternoon of the fourth day. We had reached the Platte River about midmorning and moved along its eastern bank until we passed Grand Island and approached the fort.

In a group conference that morning, we had decided the rest of us would continue along the river while Dad rode into the fort to get any news. As soon as Fort Kearny was sighted, he trotted off, leaving us to amble along beside the Platte. In the spring of each year, rain and melting snow pushed the river's current well above its banks. By early summer, most areas formed shallow creeks flowing eastward around numerous islands and sandbars. Since we were now well into the heat of summer, the Platte lay almost dry in many places.

Dad knew Fort Kearny, as he had visited there on our way to North Dakota just last year. U.S. Army Lieutenant Daniel P. Woodbury constructed the fort in 1848 and named it for Colonel Stephen

W. Kearny. Somewhere along the line, *Kearny* had been changed to *Kearney*. Never much of a fort, in 1853 the post consisted of some mud or adobe and some wooden buildings armed with a few artillery pieces. I remember reading about the fort from an 1857 first-hand account (see my third adventure in time narrative) and could tell it was quite accurate even from a distance.

I noticed James and Dad conferring before he rode off. When I inquired of James as to the subject, he just shrugged and moved away. Dad returned much sooner than any of us expected, and told us many of the soldiers in the fort were ill with what might have been cholera or dysentery. I'd read about these diseases. Most often caused by bacteria in contaminated food or water, they caused bloody diarrhea and often killed their victims. Mom and Nellie now declared we would drink no water that had not been boiled first. Not being allowed to camp within three miles of the fort, we pushed on until dark.

Each day, day after day, we proceeded west along the south bank of the Platte, as the river meandered northward. One day turned into another. Everything the same and everything different. I drove or walked mile after mile and became thinner and more muscular. Baidepe walked or rode with James and Nellie. In the evenings, Mom used some of the calico to make the girl some simple shift dresses. Baidepe refused to wear what Mom called *pantaloons*, a long-legged panty-like garment. Baidepe learned words quickly and soon could be relied upon to understand simple requests. She helped Nellie with chores, turned the spit over the fire, and carried water and firewood. She created a slingshot from a scrap of leather and a branch from a cottonwood tree. She could bring down a rabbit with one fierce, accurate shot.

I began to do as many previous travelers had done—to count graves. Some days we passed twenty or more. I knew a cholera epidemic had killed hundreds between 1849 and 1854. I saw marked graves, unmarked graves, and graves disturbed by carnivores. I sometimes saw bones scattered around with bits and pieces of flesh and cloth still attached. I worried about Mom, knowing she was not feeling well. Strange, since her occupation required her to do strenuous labor in the summer months. Dad sometimes made her ride in the wagon during the heat of the day to nap. I don't know if she actually slept, as a moving wagon, across what was now a wagon-worn trail, bumped and rocked along. Nellie, like Mom, had lost weight; we all had, except Baidepe. After a week or so, she no longer looked like a walking skeleton.

I also counted wolves. Rarely did a day pass that I didn't count at least one wolf, always in the distance, just like the many American Indians we all saw on hillsides or crossing the river farther upstream or downstream. No matter how deserted the land seemed to be, there were people there, Native peoples, soldiers from nearby forts, and travelers going east from California or Oregon. Sometimes, these eastward travelers would camp nearby, while at other times after a brief conversation and information about what lay ahead, they would continue their journey.

Although Baidepe hid when strangers appeared, she seemed to like everyone except me. She ignored me, refused to speak to me, and even turned away when I spoke to her. I soon got used to being scorned. I did discover how she watched for my return when I was away from camp, but would immediately turn her attention to some task when I rode back into camp.

"Mom, do you have any idea why Baidepe doesn't like me?"

"Greg, my best guess is it's a cultural thing. In some tribes, girls are not allowed to acknowledge or associate with older boys, even their older brothers. Perhaps that's the case here."

"Oh, strange."

We crossed the South Platte at Ash Hollow, bringing us into the North Platte river valley. After the crossing, we climbed a steep hill, which some pioneers called California Hill, to the top, a plateau or flat-topped hill, and then proceeded back down

Windlass Hill. We needed Budweiser, along with the oxen, attached to each of the wagons to pull them up California. We used Budweiser as a brake going down Windlass Hill. Thousands of previous wagon wheels had carved deep grooves into the sandstone of the California and Windlass hills. We camped at Ash Hollow for an extra day after crossing the river and climbing up and down the plateau, as the hollow contained lots of grass and fresh water. The crossing itself had been uneventful since the Platte ran low at this point in the summer.

Another thirty miles and two days brought us to Courthouse Rock and Jail Rock. These large formations, once part of an eroded plateau, jut into the sky above Pumpkin Creek. I had seen such formations before in the west, but these two became prominent landmarks for the Oregon Trial. Made of red sandstone, Courthouse Rock is imposing and looks like a large public building—you know, like a courthouse. Jail Rock is smaller, and from a distance, the two seemed to be one. We all took the time to ride out to the formations and check them out. The red sandstone formations were massive, with steep sides that up close looked like tightly-packed sand castles. You could see crystals of clear quartz and flakes of mica, a mirror-like rock, in the sandstone.

Next came Chimney Rock, another formation, this time with a spire on the top, hence the name. Like the first two, it stands off the river some ways, the distance quite deceiving in the summer heat. Another twenty miles or so and we passed Scott's Bluff, a series of bluffs or steep hills located on the south side of the North Platte. Some travelers counted this as one-third of the way to Oregon, while others put the measurement at Fort Laramie.

Moving along the North Platte a couple of days later, we passed that fort. I remembered reading how Fort Laramie stood at the junction of the Laramie and North Platte rivers. Built of two feet thick and twelve to fourteen feet high walls of adobe, the fort's center square was ringed by dwellings and barracks, store rooms, a blacksmith's shop, a carpenter's shop, and offices. Two entrances with heavy wooden gates, one each on the north and south walls, stood open. On the east wall, an additional enclosure held the stable and corral. Like at Fort Kearny, Dad visited the fort alone. This time, he came back with a bit of information about the destruction at Baidepe's village. The post commander had relayed how the Osage had most likely raided the Pawnee village in retaliation for a raid on an Osage camp by the Pawnee the previous summer. He also reported on the presence of some Indian warriors, hunting for game, mainly buffalo, just to the northwest of the fort.

While crossing the Laramie River, we encountered our first Indian-managed ferry. Most ferries we had encountered were owned and managed by white men. We didn't know if the Pawnee man owned the ferry, but he spoke very good English and seemed quite friendly. The fee of one dollar per wagon was one Dad quickly paid. Loaded on the ferry, our wagons and the buckboard passed over safe and dry. Mom and Nellie rode the ferry over as well. For some reason known only to her, Baidepe lay hidden in James' wagon. Dad, James, and I drove the horses and cows across the river. Not being our first river crossing, this one passed without incident.

Twenty-three days had passed between Fort Kearny and Fort Laramie. That first day in 1853, as we searched the wagons, we had discovered a calendar. One of us marked off the day each evening. Today was July 11th. Dad judged our rate of travel to be better than most trains, yet most pioneer wagon trains passed Independence Rock about the 4th of July. We still needed to travel about 200 miles before we reached that milestone.

About one week after passing Fort Laramie, still along the Platte River, Dad decided we needed a break. We had driven our oxen and horses hard, and they needed grass and rest. Finding a small, isolated canyon, we set up camp. Here, the fairly shallow North Platte contained numerous small islands, many with stands of oak, cedar, ash, and some cottonwood trees. Dad and I rode horseback out to one such island and gathered a large amount of firewood. Mom and Nellie washed clothes and aired bedding. James shot a small antelope, and Nellie planned to fry up antelope steaks for dinner.

I talked Dad into letting me ride Biscuit upstream to look for more game while he turned back toward camp. About two miles upstream, I came upon a bison herd crossing the Platte. There seemed to be thousands of them, as far as I could see, bison after bison after bison. I sat and watched as bison wandered quietly across the river. Mothers with nursing young, old bulls, older calves, and more, and more, and more. The Pirate may have thought he was punishing us by sending us back into this time, but here and now, I could forgive him. I relished the sight, one I knew would soon be impossible to see, when in the coming years, buffalo hunters killed off many of the remaining herds for skins and just to be killing.

I didn't shoot a bison, as I had no idea how to slaughter something that large. Instead, I rode back toward camp, empty handed.

Along the way, somehow, I lost that moment of joy at seeing the bison. I began to realize how much I missed Boone and Rose. I thought about the days of boredom, the constant work, thirst, wind, sun, and loneliness. Each and everything I missed edged closer and closer to the top of my consciousness as I rode back into camp. As the ride progressed, my dark mood deepened.

Back at camp about mid afternoon, Mom questioned me. "Greg, is something bothering you?"

"Yeah, I'm bored, angry, lonely, and hating this whole damn trip," I shouted.

Ignoring my use of the word *damn*, Mom began, "Son, I know this is hard . . ."

"Hard? No, impossible. I can't believe this has happened. How can you and Dad and the Jacksons just keep going? Don't you want to go back to our time? We don't belong here. I want my bed, my sneakers, a cheeseburger, ketchup, a Cookies & Creme candy bar, a computer, and Boone." My anger rose. Not wanting to be around anyone, I grabbed Biscuit's reins, vaulted onto his back, and rode out of camp, quickly urging him to a full gallop.

I rode along the Platte for what seemed like miles, pushing Biscuit harder and harder. Finally, when he stumbled, I came to myself and realized I was punishing Biscuit, who didn't deserve it. So I pulled him to a stop and dismounted. Holding the reins, I walked westward, farther and farther from our camp. I wasn't lost. The Platte lay there to my left, marking the trail. Head down and still angry, I don't know how long I walked before I caught a whiff of a strange and not really pleasant smell. I could see small white animals in the distance and recognized the faint sound of barking dogs.

I mounted Biscuit and moved toward the sight. Soon, I saw what appeared to be hundreds of sheep ahead of me, grazing and moving slowly west. In among the sheep, several dogs worked to keep them moving and herded together. I could see a wagon pulled by oxen and even a horse-drawn carriage in the distance, both headed west. When I arrived alongside the carriage, a girl, about sixteen or seventeen, pulled alongside me, sitting side-saddle on a fine bay mare.

"Well, hello. Where did you come from? Are you traveling alone?" she asked.

"East of here. My family is camped along the Platte, taking a day's rest."

"Kind of late starting out aren't you?"

"Yeah, it's a long story. Where are you headed?"

"Oh, William Gray is driving these sheep to Oregon. I plan to settle there. We started late after all the other wagon trains so the sheep would not eat up all the grass before the other pioneers traveled through. Where are you headed?"

"I don't think we've decided. Probably California. By the way, I'm Greg Harrison."

"Rebecca Ketcham, of Ithaca, New York."

"Are you related to Mr. Gray?"

"No, just traveling with his party. There are usually fifteen of us. Some four or five work driving the sheep."

About that time I heard a woman loudly fussing about something and saw the carriage pull to a halt. A well-dressed older woman stepped from the carriage and deposited on the ground the most exciting thing I had seen in days. I would say the loveliest, but Rebecca was mighty pretty. Squirming about in the dust of the trail, the black and white puppy smelled everything nearby before stopping to pee on a large leaf. Before anyone knew what was happening, he then took off toward the sheep and started barking.

"Not again," cried Rebecca.

I jumped from Biscuit and quickly followed the little blur into the mass of moving sheep, managing to grab him by the scruff just before one of the older dogs reached him. One of the shepherds arrived to investigate.

"Good day, I'm Hiram James. Saw you ride up and this little scamp escape from the wagon. She's trouble, she is. Too small to herd and too big to keep in the wagon. Had a litter of five the bitch did, but all the others died right off. Only one left. Mr. Gray threatens to shoot her every evening. One of these days he will."

Hiram talked as much as I do when excited.

"Uh, I'll take her. Would Mr. Gray want money for her?"

"What? NO! She's just trouble; you are welcome to her," answered Rebecca. "We'll be stopping soon. Would you like to stay for the evening meal?"

"Sorry, I need to get back, my parents will be worried. Are you sure I can keep her?"

Suddenly the older woman spoke forcibly, "Take that puppy, and I say good riddance."

So, in imitation of Dad, I doffed my hat, gave a bow, wished Rebecca and Hiram a good evening, and rode east into the rapidly increasing darkness with a puppy in my arms, feeling better than I had for days.

11
Grounded, Again!

Boy, was Mom mad when I returned. Dusk had passed, and the night, lit by only a quarter moon, was dark when I rode into camp holding my prize, with my attitude better than it had been for days. At least until Dad got hold of me. His dressing down lasted for several minutes, during which the puppy peed all down the front of my pants. Then Mom got up from her stool next to the campfire, walked over, handed me a full plate of food, took the puppy, and walked off without a word. I felt miserable once again.

When Dad finally calmed a bit, I apologized.

"Sit and eat while I see to Emily," and he turned and walked into the darkness.

I'll have to admit, I was starved. I'd had nothing since breakfast. The antelope steak was cold, but rich and delicious. Nellie had baked beans, made white bread, and had even found some greens that greatly resembled a salad. I scarfed it all down. James wandered over to the fire and handed me a cup of tea, sweetened with a bit of honey. By the time Dad and Mom returned I was full and content, but I knew the worst was yet to come.

They walked out from the darkness at the edge of camp with Dad holding the puppy. Mom's eyes were red from crying, and she carried one of Dad's handkerchiefs.

"I'll look after Biscuit," stated James. He left holding a curry comb in one hand and the reins in another.

"Okay, son. Explain what's going on, and how you managed to find a puppy out the middle of the Wyoming Territory."

I told the entire story; the bison herd, my feelings about being stuck here in 1853, my desire to go home to my own time, and my worries about all of us, our future, and Rose and Boone. When I finished, I told about riding along the Platte and seeing the flock of sheep about ten miles ahead of us.

"Yeah, I knew we were following a flock. I've noticed the lack of grass for about a week now. That's one reason I decided to stay here and graze our animals for a day or two. I didn't realize we were following so closely behind."

"Rebecca said there were about a thousand sheep and four or five shepherds, plus a party of about eleven men and women. They, the sheep, belong to a Mr. William H. Gray. He's taking them to Oregon. This is his second or third trip. Anyway, one of the female dogs had five puppies, and only this one lived. She caused quite a stir while I was talking with Rebecca, and she said Mr. Gray wanted to shoot her, I mean the puppy, not Rebecca. So, I volunteered to take her off their hands. Really, Mom, they were glad to see her go. She kept running into the flock and causing all kinds of mischief."

"Who is this Rebecca?" asked Mom.

"Oh, she's about a year or so older than me and is traveling with the Gray party, on her own. She has no family. She rode up on a pretty bay mare and talked to me. Oh, her last name is Ketcham, and she's from Ithaca, New York."

"Seems you learned quite a bit about this young lady in a short period of time? I assume she's pretty?" joked Dad.

Mom punched him in the arm, saying, "Ken, stay on topic!"

The questions continued. James returned, and he, Baidepe, and Nellie went to bed. At some point, Mom handed me the puppy again, and again, she peed all over my pants.

"Change your clothes. You can scrub those in the morning before we pull out. I suggest you find a rope and make some sort of collar for that puppy. Then go to bed. You're grounded," Mom snarled, and off she marched to their wagon.

"Ah . . . , Dad, how can I be grounded?"

"Greg, your mother is very, very upset. She was terrified when you rode off alone and stayed away so long. She's furious with me for not going after you, steamed with James for suggesting we let you work this out on your own, jealous of Nellie for being happy about having Baidepe, and well, other things have her concerned about our future. My suggestion for you is to try *toeing the line* around her for the next week or so. She'll calm down at some point. She always does."

She didn't. I tried. Really, I did. I made sure to take care of the puppy and all the animals every day without being asked. I did little things like bringing her wildflowers. I even found some late blackberries and brought a hat-full back to camp. I figured a blackberry cobbler would cheer her up. Instead, I got a lecture on grizzly bears and berries.

Mom has never been one to complain, but one day, after tripping over her long skirt while trying to carry water, she lost it. I've never heard her so angry. In the end, she pulled off the skirt and her petticoat and marched back to their wagon in her pantaloons. By the way, mid-1800s pantaloons are not sewn together in the crotch like panties, and her bum showed the entire way. They're made that way so ladies can go to the bathroom without having to pull them down. As Mom marched across our camp, Dad laughed, which made her even more angry. When she stepped down from the wagon an hour or so later for dinner, we all got a shock. Mom had created herself a pair of what could be called loose trousers. They flared out at the hips, like jodhpurs, with bands that buttoned at the ankle.

"Don't you dare laugh, not one of you. These are called bloomers and became quite the rage of the women's suffrage movement of the early 1850s. If Amelia Bloomer, Fanny Kemble, and Lizzie Cady Stanton can wear them, then so can I," and she marched over to the fire, poured herself a cup of coffee, and settled on a stool. She had fashioned her bloomers from her former skirt. She looked very funny, but quite comfortable.

"Emily, will you make me a pair as well?" asked Nellie.

"First thing tomorrow," Mom replied laughingly, and just like that, her mood lifted, and things settled back to normal. Mom and Nellie continued to wear their modified bloomers for the remainder of the trip. Mom even made them each a pair from some of the wool. The wool being various colors of plaid, their bloomers looked even more ridiculous, but Mom declared them warm and suitable. None of us, not even Dad disagreed or laughed.

We had passed the Gray party the day after I got the puppy. I'd had only a minute to speak with Rebecca, being grounded and such. Once we were ahead of the flock, the grass situation improved some, but still we often struggled to find a decent camping place in the evening. At each camp, we needed water, grass, and security. Land directly around the Platte or its tributaries continued to be green and somewhat lush; yet, as soon as you left this swath across the landscape, you encountered dry soil, mountains, and tall bluffs, often covered in names written in axle grease. Mom refused to let me contribute to this early graffiti, so I remained an unknown traveler on the Oregon Trail.

In the evenings, we took to playing chess or English *draughts*, what we call checkers. We even held tournaments. James often won at checkers, but Mom beat us all at chess. We also found playing cards, and I learned several poker games, including five card stud. Otherwise, my evenings often involved trying to housebreak a puppy. It's hard when you don't have a house.

We crossed and recrossed the North Platte several times, each time fording at low crossings. I began to think this river never ended.

12
Following the Clues

Those next weeks became agonizing. Daddy and I settled in at the ranch. I absolutely refused to leave. Daddy suggested we may have to move somewhere else if the Harrisons and Jacksons continued to remain missing. Each day, I fed the animals and mostly rode aimlessly about the ranch. Melissa left after about a week. One of Emily's staff took over the excavations at the archaeological site. For now, her crew left all of the artifacts and analysis at the ranch in Emily's office. We talked with Sam or John every day to get an update. The FBI joined in the hunt. Seems everyone was being questioned, and there was an all-out manhunt for the Pirate and his accomplice. Of course, the poor FBI doesn't know about anyone's ability to time travel! It was a disaster.

Sam and John believed my involvement with the Pirate also put me at risk of kidnap, so two other STTIU agents remained at the ranch as bodyguards.

Finally, on July 10th, John and Sam arrived with Ken's plane. The STTIU had replaced the plane's front tire and flown it to another airport, where it was thoroughly searched. After finding no clues as to what happened, they decided to return it to the ranch. Daddy and I spent the following morning removing all the personal belongings from the plane and putting them away. We had planned to go into Medora for supplies in the afternoon. Daddy can't fly a plane, so the trip took up the remainder of the day. Just before we left for Medora, I found Greg's cell phone tucked inside one of the suitcases, but the battery was dead, of course. I placed it on the charger in his room.

Early the next day, I remembered Greg's phone and retrieved it. I entered his pass code— Boone's birth date. Immediately, I noticed the note function was still open and I read. *PIRATE*. "Duh, Greg, we had already figured that out. Couldn't you have given me more of a clue?" I thought.

I showed Daddy the message, and he called Sam. The agents had never been able to access the phone after finding it jammed into one of the seats, but it made little difference, as we already figured the Pirate was responsible.

On the morning of July 12th, I opened a map and looked up the exact location of their disappearance. Except for some ranches and the airport, the area appeared to be nothing more than prairie. I sat and stared at the map for what seemed like hours. About midday, Daddy received a call from Sam. Their Internet security team had identified two names in a message, *St. Louis* and *Independence.* Their techs continued to try and hack into the Pirate's messages to discover more, and Sam promised to keep us informed.

After Daddy and I received the message, we both stared at the map. St. Louis sits due east of Independence, which is now just a suburb of Kansas City. Both cities are located on the Missouri River. With my finger, I followed the Missouri north and slightly west out of Kansas City. That took me to Omaha. I traced back and looked at the map again, planning to start again at St. Louis. Daddy stared over my shoulder the entire time, watching and thinking.

Suddenly we both shouted, "The Oregon Trail, they're on the Oregon Trail!"

"That makes sense. The Pirate did to them what we did to him. He sent them back in time on the Oregon Trail. Ken said the Pirate had never harmed anyone before he stabbed Emily. Even Emily said she thought he hadn't meant to harm her, he only wanted to keep her from time jumping. He planned to just tie her up and wait for Ken to arrive. The same with Greg and me. He only shot to stop us from jumping. I think he only planned to scare us, not to wound Greg," I rambled, quite proud of my new theory.

"I like it, sounds good, but why . . .. Why?" Daddy asked.

"Okay, look at it this way. The Pirate and his accomplice kidnap them all. He makes them time jump to a place on the Oregon Trail. He provides them with money or supplies or both to go west. Now, they have no artifacts from our time, so they can't come back. No one can find them. Oh, and he's free to steal as much from history as he can. Why send them west? Well, first they are more unlikely to find another time traveler from our time in the unpopulated West."

"Let's call Sam and see what he thinks of our theory," suggested Daddy.

Right as Daddy reached for the phone, one of the bodyguard agents called from Ken's office, "Rose, can you come in here a moment?"

When I reached Ken's office, he pointed to the computer screen and asked, "Have you ever seen this woman?"

"Sure, she's the STTIU agent who followed me from the Denver airport to New York. I didn't speak with her, but she followed my every move. Kind of annoying being watched like that," I answered.

"Uh, Rose, Mr. Engram, this woman is not a STTIU agent. Right now we believe she's the Pirate's accomplice. Sam just sent me this picture."

"Call Sam, please. We have a theory," Daddy requested.

The next bit took several minutes, as Sam told us how they had found the woman's picture on airport security videos and realized she was following me. They had earlier discovered how the agent who should have been escorting me had been called off at the last minute and told to report to another assignment in a different time. This all came to light when they discovered the STTIU's Internet connection had been hacked.

Finally, Daddy and I told Sam our theory.

"Perhaps, but don't you think it's a reach? We have no proof of any such plan by the Pirate. I think it's more likely they were killed and buried in some previous time," Sam answered grimly.

"No, no, no!" I ran screaming to my room. "They are not dead."

13
Traveling On

The terrain became more rocky day by day. We passed Register Cliff, where pioneers had once again etched their names into the rocks. Our rate of travel slowed considerably. Sometimes we made only ten to twelve miles per day. The distance from Fort Laramie to Independence Rock, some 200 or so miles, took us three weeks. Back in our time, we could have traveled the distance in about three and one-half hours. A few days before reaching this significant milestone, we passed the grave of Joel Hembree, the oldest known grave on the Oregon Trail. Six-year-old Joel died on 18 July 1843 after slipping off a wagon tongue and being run over by the wagon's wheels. A young doctor, Marcus Whitman, tended to Joel, but nothing could be done. His family buried him in a dresser drawer and carved his name and death date on a marker. A fellow traveler in the same wagon train wrote of the incident in his journal, helping to identify the young boy when his grave was rediscovered in 1961. I remembered reading the story. That night at supper, I told the story and urged Nellie and James to keep an eye on Baidepe.

The first of August—a day that will live in our memories for so many reasons—began hot and got hotter. Dad shot three rattlesnakes before breakfast, and James stepped on another one. Luckily for him, it was a young one; its strike only hit the heel of his boot. The real damage from the incident fell on Nellie, for when James, startled by the snake let out a mighty yelp, Nellie spilled boiling coffee on her arm and hand. Mom and I rushed to her side. Nellie sat sobbing and holding her quickly blistering hand. Dad came over and shot the snake while it was still attached to James' boot. Baidepe ran for water from the nearby Sweetwater River. James rushed to their wagon and returned with the same medicine box Nellie had found on our first day in 1853. It wasn't much help.

Baidepe stuck Nellie's hand in the cold river water and then began rummaging through the box of cooking goods next to the fire. Mom and Nellie, who was quietly sobbing in pain, both tried to think of what to use for a dressing, having no aloe vera or slippery elm, another early remedy for burns. Baidepe pulled the small jar of honey from the box. After dabbing Nellie's arm and hand dry with the edge of a clean cloth Mom had produced, Baidepe spread the burned skin with honey.

"I remember now. All sorts of primitive peoples used honey as a salve, especially unprocessed raw honey like this," Mom stated.

"It feels much better," Nellie answered while using her other arm to give Baidepe a hug.

Mom found bandages in the medicine box and bound Nellie's arm and hand. "No more work for you. Just sit and try to relax. There's a bit of laudanum in here if you need it later for pain."

James sat down and pulled off his boot. The dead snake was still attached by its fangs. He wrenched it off and started to throw it away, then hesitated and instead skinned the snake and attached its skin to the side of their wagon. "Since he tried to do me in, I think I'll just make a hat band from the little fellow once he dries out."

About an hour later, we finally got underway. Nellie rode in their wagon while James walked alongside, driving their oxen. I noticed she had her arm in a sling and cushioned on a pillow. Nellie wanted Baidepe to ride with me in the buckboard, so as to avoid snakes. Of course, Baidepe, who wanted nothing to do with me, refused. So, in order to make most everyone happy, Mom drove the buckboard while Dad drove our wagon, and I had a day on horseback. This made everyone happy except Becky. Oh, that's what I named the puppy. Still too young to walk, or be trusted to walk, all day, she was restricted to sitting, tied, of course, on our wagon's seat.

I chose Clown, and off we rode into a narrow river valley in the Rattlesnake Hills. I saw, but avoided, three more of those dangerous snakes before midmorning.

The day's temperature continued to rise, I think I said that before. By midday we could see Independence Rock wavering in the distance, looking like some kind of massive structure. We also saw Indians. All day long, they appeared on hillsides, on the other side of the river, and in groves of trees. Sometimes there would be one or two, at other times groups of ten or more, just sitting on their horses and watching us pass. They made me nervous, and I stayed within sight of the wagons at all times. Early on, Dad called me over with instructions. "Greg, just continue on. Keep a lookout, but don't stare or look concerned."

Right. Easier said than done.

We now traveled in Shoshone territory. During this part of the summer, the tribe's men would hunt for meat to be dried and stored for winter. We had seen large bison herds several times, but none in the last few days. About mid-afternoon, we reached Independence Rock, which looks like a giant turtle or even a whale from a distance. Thousands upon thousands of names could be seen written and carved into the red granite monolith. Mom, Dad, James, and I clambered over the feature and shouted out names we discovered. Most believe William L. Sublette, a mountain man and trader, on his way to the Wind

River range with a party of eighty-one men and ten wagons, celebrated Independence Day here in 1830.

Afterward, we camped for the night. For the first time ever, we circled the wagons, which was hard with only three. It ended up looking like an isosceles triangle with the buckboard forming the short side. During the evening, Dad and James watched our stock from horseback, and when we had finished our evening meal, we put the cows, oxen, and horses in the center of the triangle. The horses proved troublesome, especially Midnight. Finally Dad hobbled and tied him to the open side of their wagon, outside the triangle.

We divided up the overnight watch. Dad insisted I take the first few hours. We rarely kept an overnight guard, but with all the Indian activity in the area, it seemed necessary. We knew from studying history and talking with eastbound travelers, that local Indians would often steal horses and cattle from wagon trains. Dad relieved me about midnight, and James took over about four in the morning. That's when Dad discovered Midnight was gone. He - Dad, I mean - stomped, bellowed, and woke Mom, Nellie, and me, and declared he would recover the horse. We all slept about two more hours. At dawn, Dad mounted Biscuit and off he rode in search of Midnight. Before he rode off, Dad had suggested we move along. Nellie looked very tired, but insisted she could travel. So, I drove the buckboard while James and Mom drove the wagons. We tied the cows,

Clown, and Ghost each behind a wagon. The calf followed along behind its mother. We could not risk losing any more of our livestock.

Between Independence Rock and South Pass, we would need to cross the Sweetwater River about nine times, according to recent eastbound travelers we had met along the way and the guidebooks. The Sweetwater flowed east northeast along the north side of the Antelope Hills and then east-southeast between the Granite Mountains to our north and the Green Mountains to our south. While the Platte had been low all summer, the Sweetwater, fed by melting snow in the Rockies, flowed swift and deep. Following the river would bring us directly to South Pass, the easiest pass through the Rocky Mountains, a distance of about one hundred miles.

That morning I noticed how the river meandered over the landscape in great sweeping curves or bends. If we followed each curve, we would need days and days to travel to the South Pass. By crossing the river at each bend, we could cut days off our journey. Yet, with Dad out searching for Midnight, we were severely short handed. Nellie, a poor driver to begin with, was now handicapped due to her burned hand and arm. Baidepe was too small to be of much help. So, James and I decided, at least for the first day, to follow the river. We passed Devil's Gate, a natural, narrow gorge in the hills alongside the river, about midday and made about twenty miles before stopping to camp. Still no sign of Dad.

The second day passed about the same. Split Rock came into view, guiding us toward South Pass. During the night, one of our cows went missing. The following morning James searched for about an hour, but returned without our cow.

"Sorry. I lost the trail about two miles north. I believe she was stolen by Indians. Her tracks followed those of about three or more men riding unshod horses. She was probably tied and being led. I think it's best if we move on," James told us.

"I hate to move on without Ken," Mom stated, "but he told us to keep moving. I'll agree to one more day of traveling, but we will not cross the river."

Again, we stayed our course, following the bends of the Sweetwater. I saw Mom glancing over her shoulder time after time. Late in the afternoon, we reached a narrow canyon in the hills called Three Crossings. We had to make a choice—cross the Sweetwater three times within the next two miles or follow the alternate route on the south side through deep sand. Mom, James, and I discussed our options. We knew our overloaded wagons and heavy buckboard would prove exhausting if not impossible for our oxen and Budweiser.

"I think we have to make the crossings," Mom said, finally relenting and agreeing with James and me. "How about we camp here tonight, and if

Ken has not returned by dawn, we'll make the first crossing?"

"If you feel up to it, I think that should be our plan," James replied.

"What?" I asked. "Mom, are you still feeling poorly?"

"Oh, Greg, I'll explain when your Dad returns. Can you take care of the animals? I'll see to Nellie's hand and then start supper. Do we have any firewood at all, or do I have to use those awful buffalo chips?"

"We have a bit of kindling, but then it's chips. I didn't have time to pick up wood for the last few days. Really didn't see much along the way. This area has been picked clean by previous travelers," I replied and wandered off, still trying to figure out what was going on with Mom.

Nellie felt miserable, so James gave her a bit of laudanum and put her to bed. Baidepe helped with the cooking. Mom managed cornbread, beans, and bacon. She's not much of a cook under normal circumstances. As we cleaned up and tended to the animals, wolves began to howl rather close by. James and I decided to place all the animals in our little triangle and stand guard. Mom took to her bed, declaring herself to be exhausted. I stood the first watch and James the second. We kept the fire burning, using buffalo chips, and listened as wolves and coyotes hunted in the surrounding valley and hills. By morning, James and I were exhausted. However, after a good night's sleep, Mom and Nellie managed together to make a hearty breakfast that even included sourdough biscuits slathered in butter.

We loaded up and approached the first crossing. Together we'd formed a plan. James would drive his team across first. He and Nellie had worked to place their belongings up as high as possible in the wagon. While caulked and somewhat waterproof, some river water would seep in during deep crossings. James angled his oxen in, headed slightly downstream. Then about midstream, he changed direction and covered the last half going slightly upstream. Both the guidebooks, and some pioneer diaries I had perused during my study unit, suggested this method.

James crossed easily. I rode across on Ghost, the more stable of our two remaining horses, not counting Budweiser, leading Clown. Again, no problem other than arriving on the other bank cold and wet. We left Nellie and Baidepe on that side of the river, then James and I both rode back across and prepared to move our wagon over. We gave Mom the option of riding in the wagon, driving, or riding a horse across.

"Horse," she announced after some deliberation. "I'll ride Ghost, but I'll wait until you have the wagon and buckboard across."

I climbed up on Mom's wagon and took the reins just as James led the oxen down the bank and into the water. I repeated his maneuver, but midstream something happened. First, the wagon stopped, and no matter how hard our oxen pulled, it would not budge. Next, the wagon began to tilt. Just as I knew it was going to go over and had prepared to jump, I saw Mom ride up beside the wagon on Budweiser. She was on the upstream side. I don't know how she had managed to get on him, but there she sat astride his huge back. She threw me a rope, and after I tied it to a large iron hook we had used with ropes to slow the wagon on California and Windlass hills, Mom rode the rest of the way across and tied the rope to the back of James' wagon. While our wagon continued to list downstream, I didn't feel as if it would tilt over at any moment. James rode across on Clown and helped Nellie unhitch their oxen. Soon James led Lefty and Righty down to the bank and rode out with yet another rope, tying it to Big Brown's yoke. All of this took about a quarter of an hour. Using Lefty and Righty, James urged my wagon forward. Seems I had simply, and unknowingly, driven into a cleft in the river's rock bottom. Once pulled free, our oxen hauled the wagon on across. That still left the cows, Ghost, and the buckboard on the other side. Once more, riding Budweiser and Clown, James and I crossed the Sweetwater going east.

We re-hitched Budweiser and tied Ghost to the back of the buckboard, and off I rode again, into the river. By now my teeth chattered, and my feet felt frozen. The buckboard was not as tall as the wagons, so the water rose higher and higher as I crossed. Finally, I reached the other bank and pulled ashore. Behind me Ghost snorted and pulled at the rope. The cows simply swam across and began eating grass. James arrived last on Clown. One crossing completed, and we had at least two more ahead of us that day.

Still within view of Split Rock, a massive cleft in a nearby rock formation, I sat and wondered what was to become of us. Without Dad's guidance and help, we were in a precarious situation. Nellie's hand and arm remained bandaged and unusable. Baidepe was only a child. Mom seemed tired and weak for the first time I could ever remember. That left James and me, still healthy and strong, to carry out most of the work. After a brief talk, James suggested I ride ahead and see if a good camping spot existed after only one more crossing. In the meantime, he would re-harness all our draft animals, check on Nellie and Mom, and try to move ahead. It would be slow going, as Nellie would have to drive the buckboard. Budweiser most always just followed along after the two wagons, so she could easily drive with only one useful hand.

I took Clown and started off. The next crossing came in about half a mile and lay between two steep rock walls called the Narrows. I crossed the river once again, found a likely camping spot, and returned to our wagons. Areas of deep sand would have to be avoided, but I believed we could make one more crossing that day, before dark, if we hurried.

We barely made it. Then, surrounded by tall rock cliffs on two sides, we made our fire, and hung our wet clothing to dry. With the livestock inside our little triangle, we bedded down. Mom and Nellie took first watch. James took the middle of the night, leaving me the last few hours including dawn. So, I was awake when Dad splashed across the Sweetwater riding Midnight.

"Morning son, got any hot coffee?" he asked.

"Dad, how did you get ahead of us? Where's Biscuit? Where have you been?"

"Later, Greg, I'll tell you all about it later. Right now I'm starving, cold, and wet. So, about that coffee?"

14
Rose's Plan

"Daddy, I have an idea, but I'll need your help," I whispered. With our two bodyguards always nearby, Daddy and I had learned to whisper or use text messages on our phones when we wanted to communicate privately.

"Okay, how about we announce we're going for a ride? Then we can at least be far enough away from whoever follows us to talk quietly?" Daddy whispered back.

About half an hour later, with Boone running along beside us, Daddy, on Greg's horse Cody, and I, on Mattie, rode west out of the paddock. Our bodyguard was still mounting Little Blackie, the horse that once belonged to the Pirate. We got about one quarter of a mile ahead before he even came into sight.

"I want to go to Nebraska to where they disappeared and take a coin from every year from 1840 to 1865. Then we can jump back and look around for clues," I suggested.

"Since you have obviously given this some thought, any idea what we might be looking for?"

"Yep. I think we might find a campfire or wagon tracks. I mean, I don't think they would have left immediately if the Pirate gave them horses or wagons. They would have considered their options, made plans, and started out the next day." Daddy started to interrupt me, but I held up my hand palm first to forestall him. "Just hear me out. They started out from a place that was only prairie, not on the actual Oregon Trail. They would have most likely left some kind of evidence. If we can find a clue, any clue, in any given year, we can then move westward along the Oregon Trail by car and jump back at various places, especially at the forts and other places where traders might have encountered them. It's worth a try, and I can't just sit here and do nothing. We'll need mid-1800s clothing and some good maps. I've already downloaded all of the historic ones I could find online."

"Rose, where will we get the coins and clothing? I don't know if the STTIU will give us those things, since they consider our theory to be unlikely."

"Well, I haven't figured out all of the coin part yet, but we might improvise the clothing."

"Let me give this some consideration. For now, keep working on those maps."

We finished our ride, and when we returned to the ranch house, we found Sam and John waiting for us.

I remained furious with them both and didn't want to speak with either, but Sam's first words somewhat changed my opinion of him.

"Matthew, Rose, I want to apologize for my previous blunt statement. John and I have looked at the disappearance based on the facts we have at hand and your knowledge of the Pirate. Rose, you're right. He's deliberately harmed no one in the past. I – no, we - think Ken's and James' aggressive tactics to stop the Pirate forced him and his crew into a desperate act to take Ken and James out of their path to stealing more historic artifacts. We believe the Pirate's crew is planning a 'find' of massive importance and value. So, we would like to take you both to the airport where the families were abducted and start a time search. Hopefully, we'll find evidence they are alive and not their bodies. But either way, at least we'll know," Sam explained.

"When can we leave?" I urged.

"Tomorrow. We brought along coins for all the years from 1830 to 1900, some nineteenth-century clothing, and other supplies. We can take the plane, since John's a pilot, and be there by noon."

"I suggest we narrow down our search to 1840 to 1865, at least to start. Those are the major years the Oregon Trail was in use. I'll go pack. Oh, and we're taking Boone. He might pick up a scent as we go west," I stated.

"Go west?" questioned John and Sam together.

"Yes, after we search that area year by year and find the right year, then we'll need a car to drive west along the Oregon Trail route so we can ask at places like Fort Kearny, Fort Laramie, and Fort Bridger. I have some maps already marked up and have figured out their rate of progress based on twelve to fifteen miles per day. By now, they must be well past Fort Laramie, somewhere between there and South Pass. I'll show you the maps after dinner," I stated hurriedly while leaving the room. "I'm going to pack my things, including my laptop. Can we fit Boone's crate in the plane? We might need it later in the trip. Can you see to that, Daddy?" And with that, I left them all sitting open mouthed and staring.

"Matthew, your daughter is quite something! Someday she'll rule the world," John remarked, as I left the room.

"No doubt she will. She's way ahead of you both!" Daddy retorted with a smile.

So the next morning, while John worked through the preflight checklist, we finished packing the plane. Boone doesn't like Sam and John much, but Daddy got him into the plane and into his crate. We'd decided Boone would be safer that way, as we had strapped his crate into the space behind the two rear seats. We left about 8:00 a.m. and arrived at the small rural airport just a little after noon. The airport was busy, so we could not start our search immediately. Two small planes were being readied for take off, and a Piper Cub zoomed overhead with a student and a flying instructor. John and Sam decided it would be best if we topped off our fuel and made a bathroom stop. Then, we could return later in the day.

Daddy asked the airport manager questions about times when lessons took place, pretending to be interested in learning to fly, but actually just trying to find out when the airport would be deserted. Off we went into Kansas City, rented a large car and a travel trailer that sleeps four, loaded up, and started our drive back to the little airport. Along the way, we grabbed a late lunch and some food for the coming days. When we arrived the second time, almost at dusk, the airport stood deserted and quiet.

I walked Boone, and then Sam, Daddy, and I changed into our nineteenth-century costumes, and prepared to jump to 1840. That's when I remembered how only Greg can transport animals through time. Our plan included John staying behind as our lookout. Now, he'd have to watch after Boone, who would be of no use at all.

Daddy, Sam, and I jumped. The prairie appeared empty. We walked a grid pattern for almost an hour before it became too dark to see much at all. We jumped back, made dinner, and worked on our plan of action.

Later, I wandered about the airport. One of the hangar's side doors was unlocked, and I let myself in. I had a flashlight, and I wandered around the space, just looking and thinking. I was almost back to the door, after making a complete circle inside the hangar, when something caught my eye. There, next to the door, lying in a pile of dust and debris, lay Greg's woven leather bracelet with this year's coin still hidden in its secret pouch. I picked it up and brushed away the dust and dirt. Now we knew for sure, they had been forced to time jump with no way to return. I showed the bracelet to Daddy, Sam, and John when I returned to the trailer. Yet another clue confirming our suspicions, but telling us nothing we didn't already suspect.

I cleaned the leather and placed the bracelet in my nineteenth-century skirt's hidden pocket for good luck and safe keeping.

The next morning, after a light breakfast, we once again began our search. Luckily, the airport was not busy, and we had devised a cover story for our being there. According to our "story," John was an independent film director looking for a convenient and suitable site to film a time-travel adventure film. We had parked the trailer behind the hangar, and from there could appear and disappear without anyone being the wiser—most of the time. To disguise our appearances and disappearances, John would pop into our historic time every thirty minutes, on the hour and half hour, to see if we were ready to return and let us know if the *coast was clear*, so to speak. If anyone came around asking questions, then John would not appear, and we would stay in the past until he came to get us.

That morning we searched 1841, 1842, and 1843 until the Indians appeared on the other side of the Big Blue river. So, we jumped back without waiting for John and startled both him and Boone, who was tied to the bumper of the travel trailer. After lunch, we searched 1844 and 1845 before Daddy and Sam jumped once again to 1843, found the Indians once again, and quickly jumped back. We decided 1843 would have to wait until last. One last jump to 1846 placed us right in the middle of a thunderstorm and pouring rain. We jumped back immediately, with each of us already soaked. With no additional nineteenth-century clothing, we had no option but to wait until the following day. So we changed, hung our wet clothes out to dry, and turned in early.

The stiff breeze across the surrounding prairie dried our clothing overnight, leaving us prepared to return to our search. While I walked Boone, Daddy, Sam, and John discussed how long this might take. When I returned suddenly, they became quiet. "Look," I stated, "we knew this would take time and would be a long shot. But we **are not** giving up."

"Rose, Sam and I were discussing leaving you here and going back alone each time, in case we encounter more Indians," Daddy explained.

"Nope. Not happening. You can try, but I'll just jump to another year and search by myself. I'd found coins for a lot of the years before I even told you my idea. I wanted to be prepared. So, I can either go with you or alone, which will it be?" I knew defying Daddy was taking quite a risk, but I was desperate to see this plan through.

"Well, Matthew, I guess she already rules the world—at least this part of it," declared Sam.

After givng me a brief *talking to* about respect and rules, Daddy relented.

So our third day began. We started with the year 1846. Apart from finding an arrowhead with a broken arrow still attached and a much too recent campfire, we found nothing of importance. No wagon tracks. We decided the fire was much too recent to have been built by the Harrisons and Jacksons. In 1847, the weather was cool, and the wind gusted, blowing our hats off our heads and making it hard to hear each other when we walked our grid pattern. We found nothing. We finished 1848 before lunch. After lunch, the airport was busy, and we had to delay time and time again. We only managed one more year, 1849.

Right after dusk, another STTIU agent arrived with supplies including more nineteenth-century clothing, dog food, and people food. I was starving and volunteered to make supper. We had a small charcoal grill, and Daddy started a fire to grill lamb chops, while I placed a box of frozen scalloped potatoes in the oven and made a salad. Our food delivery had included an angel food cake and berries, so I placed the blackberries in a bowl with some sugar to macerate. I had learned how by watching the Food Network.

Since I cooked, Sam and John cleaned up, while I walked Boone. He still didn't take to Sam and really disliked John. Later I climbed into my bunk with my Kindle and read more about the Oregon Trail. I fell asleep wondering where Greg was and if he was safe.

Jim Bridger

15
Ken's Adventure

I guess Mom heard his voice, because she soon appeared and hugged Dad like he had been gone for years. After all his adventures into the past, for years and years, mostly as part of his job, I always thought Mom believed him to be invincible. Apparently not. She berated him for several minutes, hugged him again, forced him first to wrap up in a blanket, and then made him go change into dry clothing. While he was changing, she stoked the fire to roaring and made him breakfast, all while asking more questions than even *I* could manage.

I took Midnight and rubbed him dry and gave him a feedbag full of oats from the buckboard. I could tell he was tired. He also had several scrapes and one long shallow cut across his rump, so I gathered up our stock of liniment and cleaned and treated each of his injuries.

When Nellie and James woke and joined us for breakfast, Dad agreed to tell his story.

"The first morning I spent most of my time trying to find a trail. With all the rock in this country, it's easy to hide or disguise tracks. Finally, about noon, I picked up the trail on the far side of a mountain stream. It was clear seven unshod horses were leading a shod horse, Midnight. At least, I hoped it was Midnight and not another stolen horse. I managed to follow the trail most of the afternoon, but I'll admit I had to double back time and time again in those rocks. About dusk, I found a rock overhang and decided to stay put until morning. I figured the Shoshone I was following would also bed down for the night, as I'd seen evidence about an hour earlier they'd killed either a deer or elk.

"So, I built a small fire under the ledge so the smoke would not rise in one steady stream and give away my hiding spot. I didn't know if they knew I was following, but didn't want to take the chance, as there was only one of me and seven of them. Consuming the food I had taken with me, I ate a cold dinner with lots of hot tea. I had just bedded down when I heard movement about fifty yards away. Unusual movement, as it was accompanied by a man singing 'Jeanie with the Light Brown Hair' by Stephen Foster. He wasn't being real quiet about it either. Soon I could smell him and hear him. I stayed still and waited, holding my loaded pistol under my blanket. Then there he stood. 'Got any coffee?' he asked.

"'No,' I answered. 'I've got tea.'

"'Tea, who carries tea out here in this wilderness? Only a pioneer would bring tea. No, its coffee or whiskey. No tea. Name's Jim Bridger.'

"'Ken Harrison's my name. You're welcome to join me, Jim Bridger.'

"'Here, have a swig, good whiskey in that flask,' he replied, sitting down and handing me his flask. He made himself quite at home.

"He smelled like he had not bathed in years. His buckskin clothing was filthy, and he was leading a pinto mare loaded with hides and pelts.

"'Where you headed, Ken Harrison? You're not by any chance chasing after those Shoshone what stole that big black stallion, are you?'

"'As a matter of fact, I am. Have you seen them?'

"'Spoke with Dancing Elk earlier this afternoon. Noticed the stallion and complimented my old friend on stealing it, since I knew it weren't no Indian pony. Dancing Elk told me the whole tale about him and his braves making themselves visible all day and then them puttin' the sneak on you during the night. Right proud, he was too.'

"'Yeah, I was standing guard, didn't hear a thing. Figured it was my responsibility to get him back. We're planning on starting a horse ranch in northern California. We planned on that stud being the start of our bloodline.'

"'Well,' said Jim softly. 'We better get some sleep then. We'll need our wits to get that horse back.'

"And with that statement, he unloaded the hides and pelts from his horse, hobbled her, unrolled his bedroll, and was soon fast asleep."

"You met Jim Bridger, the Jim Bridger, the mountain man? And what's this about a horse ranch in California?" I exclaimed.

Giving me the look, Dad took a big gulp of his coffee and continued his tale.

"The next morning Bridger and I began tracking those Shoshone warriors. Jim's a much better tracker than I am, and we followed them all morning, took a break in the early afternoon, and then moved in closer around dusk. We were only about one half mile behind them, and Jim declared us to be close enough. While I set up a cold camp, he walked the half mile right into their camp and declared he had come for supper. About two hours later, he returned with a big hunk of elk meat wrapped in bark and told me what he had discovered. He said we would need to wait several more hours.

"'Wait for what?' I asked him.

"'To put the sneak on them and get your horse back, of course' he answered. 'I traded ol' Dancing Elk my flask for this hunk of meat. Not enough in it to make them drunk, but they'll sleep a bit more soundly after passing it around. I'll get it back when we go for your horse.'

"'You mean we're going to simply sneak up, take Midnight, and get your flask back from seven Shoshone warriors? Are you crazy?'

"'I've been called worse, Mr. Harrison. Here's the way it is. If we go in and ask for that horse, they're likely goin' a shoot us both. Say instead, we sneak in real quiet like and take the horse. That'll show them we're being honorable about it all. The Shoshone and Sioux and some other tribes believe it's okay to take a horse or any livestock if they do it with skill and cunning. They don't consider it stealing. If you and me show we can be cunning, then they'll most likely not come after us. Now, that said, I do have one suggestion. Would you be willing to leave that gelding in place of the stallion? They'd see it as a sign of respect,' Jim stated.

"'Sure, I'll be okay with trading my gelding for the stallion,' I answered, feeling somewhat anxious about this plan of his.

"After creeping up to about fifty yards from their camp, we waited until near to an hour or so before dawn. While I moved to where their horses were tied, Jim moved toward their camp. We had already established a plan of escape. I had muzzled Biscuit with my bandana and silently led him up to Midnight, where I tied Biscuit in his place. Then I walked Midnight some distance from camp, saddled him, and mounted up. Before I even heard him approach, there stood Jim holding his flask and his horse. We moved away from their camp, assuming we had successfully escaped unheard. We had only ridden for about a minute when we heard the shout, 'Jim Bridger, you owe me one elk for that flask. You can have the black horse, he trouble. Tell that pioneer my squaw like this horse.'

"Jim laughed and laughed, but urged me to move faster. He took the lead, and we moved farther into the mountains, often walking in rocky stream beds and over rocky scree fields below steep cliffs. We traveled all morning. About noon, Jim led us into a dark cave and unsaddled his horse. After a cold lunch on the leftover elk, we both napped and let our horses rest.

"'Ken, most likely we lost those Shoshone, but just in case, I suggest we move farther on up into the mountains to another pass I know. From there you can double back along the river and meet up with your party.'

"I had told him previously you would move on through the Sweetwater River crossings.

"So, late in the afternoon, we saddled up and moved on. Jim talked constantly about all his encounters with various Indian tribes. He was just relaying one story about being trapped by over one hundred Cheyenne warriors in a box canyon when an arrow whizzed across Midnight's rump, causing him to rear up. By the time I had him under control, Jim had pulled his rifle and gotten off a shot. We quickly took cover behind some large rocks, and waited. And waited. About dusk, I whispered to Jim, 'What happened when you were trapped by those Cheyenne?'

"'They kilt me, of course,' he whispered back, chuckling.

"We stayed hidden all night, taking turns keeping watch.

"The following morning Jim woke me and declared that whomever shot the arrow was long gone, and we'd better move out. Seems he had risen earlier and scouted the area. We rode a short time and came to a narrow pass. From there, Jim pointed me southeast toward the Sweetwater. He rode off southwest toward Fort Bridger. I made it down the mountains about dark, slept for a few hours, and then started east along the river. I figured you'd be further along than you are. I'll admit, my whole return trip was slow going, as Midnight and I are both *tuckered out*, as Jim would say."

We spent most of breakfast telling Dad the story of our first crossing. I noticed he kept looking at Mom. Once the oxen were hitched, and we were ready to move out, he pulled her and me aside.

"Greg, it's time you knew. Emily's expecting a baby. You're going to have a baby brother or sister in about five months." When I didn't respond, he continued, "So, I'll need you to help me make sure from here on out that she takes it easy."

Not knowing exactly what to say to this news, I just walked over to the buckboard and harnessed Budweiser.

"Greg," Mom whispered, after following me. "I know this is a shock. We weren't sure before we left home, so we didn't tell you. Then, once we were here, we didn't know how to tell you."

"Words, Mom. You just needed to use your words. I'm fourteen. I can understand English." I left her standing there as I mounted Clown and moved out toward the next Sweetwater crossing.

All day, that's all I could think of. My mother was pregnant. After fourteen years of being an only child, I was getting a sister or brother. I worried about Mom, stayed mad at Dad for not telling me sooner, and felt scared. What if the baby came before we reached wherever we were going? Would Mom and a baby be added to those many graves beside the trail? Did Nellie know how to deliver a baby? I sure didn't, and I doubted Dad or James did.

We crossed the Sweetwater River, the final crossing in Three Crossings Canyon. A small stream ran into the Sweetwater not long after the crossing, creating a swampy area filled with ice. I had read about Ice Slough, so we used a shovel from the buckboard and dug up chunks of clear ice and placed them in a barrel we had emptied and in our water barrels. I would have given anything if we could have made ice cream!

Dad and James wanted to make three crossings that day. We were traversing an area called Rocky Ridge. The middle crossing of the day proved treacherous and took several hours. With one more before us, and that one several miles ahead, we set up camp. It was James who came over to talk with me.

"Greg, can we talk?"

"Sure."

"Your Mom and Dad are worried about your reaction to their news. Ken knows you're worried about your Mom. So, I suggested we have a camp meeting tonight and talk out our plans for the future. Your opinion counts as much as any of ours. Can you do that, come and talk to us?"

"Yeah, it's about time we all started talking to each other."

As we sat down to eat elk steaks, beans, and biscuits, Dad started off. "Okay, James and I think California should be our new home. We have Midnight, two mares, and some gold. I estimate we have enough to buy some land or establish a homestead. We might have to homestead and then register our claim. The Compromise of 1850 allowed California to enter the Union as a free, non-slavery state in September of that year. So James and Nellie won't have to worry about not having papers stating they're free Negroes. If we can buy land under my name and James' to establish a ranch, we can do so without worrying about any laws and segregation. California already has Spanish, American Indian, and even Chinese landowners and laborers. So, I suggest we work together and start a horse ranch. We're all familiar with horses. What we don't know, we can learn. Oh, and I believe we can make it to California before the baby arrives."

"So we're going to become ranchers? In California? Is there no hope for returning to our time?" I asked.

"I don't think so," replied James. "I know the STTIU had been working on a plan to place the current year's coins in various places all across the United States. That way anyone stranded in time might have a chance to return to their own time, or at least close to their own time. But the plan hasn't yet been implemented."

"Oh, but that might mean in the future, we could go home?" I asked.

"Only if we knew where they were going to hide the coins. It would have to be some old building, like an old courthouse or historic house museum. They hadn't worked out all the details yet." Dad answered. "But since we are already here, we wouldn't know where the coins were hidden."

The conversation continued on and on until Mom declared she was going to bed. Nellie followed her with Baidepe, leaving us men to continue planning.

Later, I turned in, placing my bedroll beside the fire.

"Son, are we good? Are you still mad?"

"Nope, but do me a favor. Next time, just tell me. Don't keep me in suspense, worrying about Mom and our future."

"You're right, I still think of you as my little boy instead of a man. Most boys become men about eighteen years of age, but you've proved yourself over and over on this trip. From now on, no secrets."

I bundled Becky under the covers and stroked her head as I thought about our future. At times, it would be nice to be a puppy—cared for, allowed to play all day, with no worries.

16
Help Arrives

I awoke to a cloudy sky with a hint of coming rain, dressed in my nineteenth-century clothing, and took Boone for yet another walk since we can't let him run free. The airport became busy as the morning progressed. Several pilots stopped and stared before asking me lots of questions about the movie we would be making. I invented a whole plot and characters. I even explained how right now we were only filming some clips for location and setting. I expounded on how we planned to return later in the year to begin shooting the actual movie. I suggested some of them might try out as extras. I didn't consider it to be lying, just embellishing our cover story.

Once we were all up and dressed, Sam, Daddy, and I walked down to the river's edge, where we were mostly hidden, and jumped to 1850. We then walked back up to the area where the airport now stands and began our search. We finished about an hour later, after finding nothing, but John did not appear to tell us we could return to our time. We waited and waited. At last, John popped into 1850 and motioned for us to jump back.

Next to our travel trailer stood a pickup truck pulling the four-horse trailer we used at the ranch. It's a large trailer with an area in the front for two people to sleep during long overnight trips. Tied to a line and grazing peacefully stood our horses. I ran over to nuzzle up next to Mattie, my black quarter horse. Her official name is Mattie Blaylock; she's named for Wyatt Earp's second wife. Greg's bay gelding Cody nickered and moved in my direction. After I checked both over, I decided I needed answers.

"John, what's going on? Why are our ranch horses here?" I demanded.

"Rose," Daddy began, "let me explain. Two nights ago, after you went off to bed, Sam, John, and I discussed our lack of progress and how we might search farther down river if we had horses. Since none of us can transport horses through time, we needed someone who could. So, we called headquarters and discussed the problem with the director. Now, as you already know, Greg's time-travel abilities are very rare. We found out only one other person is currently known to have those abilities. Luckily, she's available. So she flew to the ranch, gathered up four of the horses, and drove down here. Come meet Maisie and Holly Stuart."

"Glad to meet you," I answered, shaking each woman's hand. Maisie stood about five feet eight inches tall and had beautiful red hair and striking green eyes. Holly was about two inches taller and had blue eyes. "Why did you bring Little Blackie instead of Wallowa, the Appaloosa?" I asked.

"Oh, Melissa asked me to look at the Appaloosa when we arrived," she replied in a lovely Scottish accent. "She's there taking care of the ranch and working on Emily's research. I checked the Appaloosa over, what did you call her?"

"Wallowa, it means winding water in Nez Perce. What's wrong with her? Could you tell?"

"Nothing serious. I'm a veterinarian and just happened to be in the States for a conference when the director called. Wallowa is expecting a foal in about six months, so I didn't believe using her for this operation was a good idea, you know, riding in the trailer for miles and miles and then time jumping. I suspect Little Blackie there is the proud papa. He's quite good natured for a stallion."

"Holly, are you also a veterinarian?" asked Daddy.

"No, I'm a ballerina with the New York Ballet Company. Unlike my sister, I can't transport animals in time. We're fraternal twins, not identical. I only came along for a chance to see the West."

"Maisie, did you bring nineteenth-century clothing?" asked Sam. "We need to get back to searching before the rain starts."

"Aye, I'll be a wee minute." And off she went to change.

"Daddy, why the horses? I'm not sure I understand"

"Rose, the river banks in this area are too high for them to have crossed easily on horses, and impossible for wagons. So Sam and I concluded they may have crossed downstream. So, we needed a way to search quickly. Also, the horses will be useful when we approach the forts later on after we find the right year."

"Oh, smart thinking."

"Yes, sometimes people other than you have good ideas," Daddy jested, poking me gently on the shoulder.

Maisie returned within scant minutes. While she was changing, Daddy and I had saddled Cody and Mattie. The plan was for Maisie and Daddy to search the river going downstream while Sam and I searched the area where the airport now stood. In order not to be seen, and not to trample any possible evidence, Maisie and Daddy rode upstream and crossed before jumping to 1851. Sam and I jumped and began our grid search. An hour later, Daddy and Maisie returned to report finding a good ford across the river, but they discovered no evidence of wagons traveling along or crossing over the river.

After a quick lunch, we searched 1852. I was becoming discouraged and had walked over to pet Mattie when Holly approached. "Rose, the STTIU director filled us in on what happened and why you're searching this area. He said you came up with the idea even before their agents did. Sounds like you're really smart. I don't believe I would have come to the same conclusion so quickly," she explained.

"I'm beginning to think we were wrong. We keep searching year by year and finding nothing. What if rain has erased all tracks and trace of them? What if I'm just wrong?" I whispered, leaning in close to Mattie and patting her neck.

"My sister has some wonderful abilities, but I have good eyesight and am diligent. So, if you have extra clothing, how about I join you and Sam?"

So we dressed Holly in my extra skirt (it was way too short on her) and blouse, tied a bandana over her hair and took her back with us to 1853. Daddy and Maisie had changed horses and already ridden off.

Sam took the northernmost area, Holly took the center, and I started at the farthest south point of our search grid. We had been walking and looking at the ground for half an hour when John appeared and handed us each a cold bottle of water, reminding us not to leave them behind in 1853. Sometimes he was just rude, and he often treated me like a child.

Just as we returned to our search, Sam called out he had found cattle poop. At least he thought it was cattle poop. Within seconds, I found wagon wheel marks, four of them, impressed in what was once deep mud. Working with Holly and Sam, the three of us located the tracks of one other large wagon and what might have been a smaller wagon. Holly found ashes from a campfire. But the most important discovery of all was a small coin from 1853, which appeared to have been dropped right on the edge of where the airport's tarmac now began. We kept looking, but found nothing else.

When Daddy and Maisie rode back into view, we excitedly showed them our finds, and Maisie identified the poop as *cow poop* and the other droppings as *horse poop*. She also identified a large hoof print as belonging to a shod draft horse. Now certain we had identified the correct year, I had adopted Greg's habit of nonstop talking when Daddy interrupted me.

"Rose, don't you want to know what we found?" he asked, breaking into my theories about Indians not having coins in 1853 and how they often punched holes in their coins to wear them as ornaments. I learned that from Emily.

"What, what, tell me?"

"About a mile west of here is a low bank ford. Maisie and I found more horse poop, probably from a draft horse, and wagon tracks in the bank. They have eroded due to recent rains, but are still visible. Rose, I think we've found them."

We all high-fived each other and took one more look around while waiting for John.

When John appeared, we showed him our evidence and then jumped back to our time. He was skeptical, but went along with our conclusions. Still only mid-afternoon, we decided to load up and move west toward Fort Kearny. Maisie drove the pickup. Since it had a crew cab, I rode with her and Holly.

Us girls had a great time talking about their life in Scotland, time travel, the Harrisons, and the Jacksons. We discussed Sam, who we all liked, and John, who none of us really liked. I felt like smiling instead of crying. Maisie and Holly asked lots of questions about Daddy and me, our past, and our life at the ranch.

We pulled into the Kearney RV & Campground about an hour before dusk. With a bit of work, John and Sam convinced them to allow us to unload the horses. Sam then put in a call to headquarters to find ranches where we could camp as we drove west. Holly, Maisie, Daddy, and I walked the horses, curry combed each, and settled them back into the trailer with bags of horse feed and fresh water. Sam and John drove into Kearney and brought back pizza for us all. We even had a campfire and roasted marshmallows to make s'mores.

After I climbed into my bunk and urged Boone up beside me, I considered how today's finds had changed our outlook.

I knew it was still a long shot that we might find them. I mean, we had all that western territory to search, and they might have encountered hostile Indians, disease, and/or accidents. What if they had turned east instead? Although, we had found where they headed west in the beginning, they may have changed their minds. What if they didn't go into any of the forts? Would they go to California or Oregon? Still, I had something I had been lacking for more than a month. I had *hope*!

The next morning, we packed up and drove north to near the entrance to Fort Kearny State Recreation Area. Then Daddy and Sam unloaded Little Blackie, Cody, and Romeo. Maisie helped saddle each. Then they jumped to 1853 and rode toward the fort. This would not have been possible without Maisie. Good thinking on Daddy's part. The rest of us expected them to be gone several hours. They were. Finally, I could see them approaching down the river path. They had jumped back in a secluded area nearer to the fort.

"Daddy, what did they say? Did they say if they came this way?" I asked before they could even dismount.

"Rose, the fort's population was struck by dysentery about the time the Harrisons would have passed here. Only one person remembered anyone who could have been them. He said a tall blond man rode to the fort alone to ask about Indians between here and Fort Laramie. The soldier I spoke with says the man was part of a small wagon train passing by. The timing is darn close, but the lieutenant who spoke with the man returned back east about a week later. So no one knows the man's name. I'm sorry. Perhaps we'll have better luck at Fort Laramie."

I knew that fort sat only about five or so hours from Fort Kearny when traveling on today's modern roads. I went back and checked my calculations. I figured the Harrisons' wagons would have reached that fort in about three weeks, so about the middle of July. As today's date was August 11th, our party would appear at Fort Laramie less than a month after the Harrisons and Jacksons passed the fort. I thought this might give us a better chance of them being remembered.

Devil's Gate on the Sweetwater River
photographed in 1870 by
William Henry Jackson

17
Crossing South Pass

Out little wagon train's next crossing of the Sweetwater occurred with little fanfare and no trouble. We then continued our travel along Rocky Ridge. Its name tells all. We made only nine miles that day, starting late and stopping early. From this point, the land rose gradually to South Pass, where we would cross the Continental Divide. On the east side of the divide, rivers flow east toward the Mississippi River. To the west of the divide, rivers flow toward the Pacific Ocean. I knew South Pass saved many miles and much misery on the trail west. When Lewis and Clark made their expedition in 1805 and 1806, they passed through the Rockies north of here in the Bitterroot Mountains (in today's Montana and Idaho). That northern pass, being higher and rougher, nearly destroyed the entire company. South Pass, known to American Indians for years and discovered by Robert Stuart and members of the Pacific Fur Company in 1812, is a gradual climb, so gradual many pioneers didn't even realize they were passing through the Rockies.

But don't let me get ahead of myself. We still had to cross the Sweetwater four more times. We traveled about sixteen miles before reaching the next crossing. Between the day's two crossings, we climbed a high hill, over it, and down the other very stony and rough side. It required great care for Dad and James to guide the oxen down without letting them get pushed by the wagons. From there the road leveled out, but still had stony ridges here and there that bounced the wagons and everything and everyone. After the second crossing with dark approaching, we once again camped for the night. Two more crossings to go. With the night, it turned cold and windy. Ice formed on the edges of small streams and water holes. I knew that as we climbed higher and higher into the Rockies, the nights would be even colder. On the eighth of August, we made the last of the Sweetwater crossings. Only ten miles to the summit of South Pass.

It may be a gradual climb, but we knew we were at a higher elevation as the day's rain fell cold, almost like sleet, at midday when we crossed through South Pass. From here we could see the Wind River Range to the north and the Oregon Buttes and Great Divide Basin to the south. The Pass itself is some thirty-five miles wide. We saw snow caps in the Wind River Range. Snow can come early here in the mountains of the west, and we still had to climb over California's Sierra Nevada Mountains where the Donner party was trapped by snow in 1846.

From here, the trail to Fort Bridger is sixty-five or so miles. We all knew we would be lucky to make Fort Bridger by August 15th. After South Pass, the land became dry and filled with little more than sage brush and dirt. Water became harder and harder to find. We struggled to find grass for our oxen, horses, and cattle. Each one now stood rail thin. We sometimes passed what early settlers called *poison water*, which was alkaline water. I had read about how many of these streams and water holes had soft banks that could trap animals, almost like quicksand. We avoided them and used the water in our barrels for our livestock and ourselves. We filled up at any decent water hole or stream crossing, although some of the water didn't taste or look at all good.

In the evenings, we fed our livestock the remaining grain we had pulled all this way in the buckboard. By now, we were low on most every food stuff we started out with. We burned sagebrush as there was no wood available. We rationed water and suffered in the heat of August as we crossed the high plains. Mom rode in the buckboard most days, but still walked about three miles when terrain was not too rough. Dad and I looked for game each day and provided our little train with a mountain goat that lasted two days. It was tough and very chewy, but any fresh meat was better than old salt bacon.

On the 14th, we woke to find two of our oxen lame, Speck and Righty. Dad speculated that their hooves might be worn or cracked or that they had vitamin deficiencies which caused lameness. There was no grass there at Dry Sandy Crossing, so staying another day to rest our oxen was out of the question. Instead, we pulled our wagon with four oxen, using Lefty in place of Speck, and pulled the Jacksons' wagon with only Short Tail and Spook. As the buckboard was now almost empty of foodstuffs and grain, we loaded some of the supplies in the Jacksons' wagon into the buckboard to lighten the weight of their wagon. We left empty barrels sitting beside the trail. Speck limped along behind us for much of the day. I rode back and checked on him several times, and he showed up at camp about two hours after we settled for the night. Righty just disappeared somewhere back on the trail. Dad and James doctored Speck's feet and wrapped them in large pieces of hide from an elk. He stank of liniment and dead elk. Still the Jacksons were two oxen short, as you can't use just one ox in a yoke. Speck followed along behind our wagons with the other cows. Over the rough ground, with only two oxen for one wagon, our rate of travel slowed to about twelve miles a day. On the sixth day after crossing South Pass, we approached the Mormon Ferry crossing at the Green River.

"I spoke with the ferryman, and they want six dollars per wagon. We can take the livestock downstream a bit, there's a place to drive them over if you don't want to pay for the ferry to take them," I told Dad after riding back from the ferry crossing on Ghost. "There's no one waiting on either side, so we can cross over whenever we're ready."

"Sure, let me discuss it with James and Nellie and Emily. We must decide who's going to do what job."

I helped myself to a leftover biscuit and headed toward the livestock to make sure we weren't missing any. Dad caught up with me in about ten minutes.

"Greg, can you take your Mom, James, and Nellie down to the ferry with the wagons? I'll stay behind. Then you can return with James after they've both crossed over safely. We'll take the livestock downstream to cross. I assume Baidepe is with Nellie?"

"Yeah, I saw her climb into Nellie and James' wagon. She had been walking."

I can't count the number of river crossings we had made before that day. Each one different and yet the same. The livestock sometimes balked at the edge, but most of the time they just swam over. This was only our fourth or fifth ferry crossing. I'd lost count. Mom took their wagon across first. About a half hour later, Nellie urged their two remaining oxen onto the ferry, and the ferryman prodded his team. Like most ferries, the ferryman used oxen or horses to pull the ropes that hauled the ferry. Back east, large pulleys and cables pulled ferries across, but here, in the west, horses or oxen and ropes were used. James left the buckboard and Budweiser tied to one of the ferry hitching posts. He grabbed Clown from me and headed back to where Dad waited with the remaining livestock.

Then Mom screamed. I looked up to see several rough-looking men riding around Mom's wagon. Each was pulling stuff out of the wagon. We had rolled up the canvas earlier, and one man daringly jumped into the bed and rummaged in the boxes of goods. I saw Mom reach for the Walter Colt pistol we kept behind their wagon's seat, but the man in the wagon pulled it from her hands and whacked her upside her head. She fell backward into the wagon bed. I pulled my pistol aimed and fired. My shot nicked one man on the leg. As I pulled my rifle, I heard the ferryman get off two shots with his rifle. The men scattered, taking with them pieces of clothing and equipment. I even saw one with a frying pan.

Without thinking, except about Mom, I jumped Ghost into the Green River. Seemed like we sank almost to my head before we surfaced, and Ghost swam for the opposite bank. I hadn't realized the current was so fast. Ghost tried to keep us moving toward the opposite shore, but soon we were carried downstream by the rushing water and pulled down by a swift undercurrent. I lost sight of the ferry and our wagon. My hands and feet became numb with the cold. I think we struggled, Ghost and I, for almost a quarter of an hour before I realized she would drown unless I let her go. Letting her go would give her a chance to make it to shore. As we passed under an overhanging limb from one of the only large trees I had seen, I grabbed a branch and pulled my feet from the stirrups at the same time. I watched as Ghost, now free of my weight, moved toward the opposite bank, the one from where we had entered the river. I held on as long as I could, and then the river once again pulled me in.

Fort Bridger in December of 1850
Lithographer James Ackerman

18
Off to the Rescue

FINALLY, at Fort Laramie we received news of the Harrisons. One officer at the fort told Daddy, Sam, and Maisie how Ken Harrison had visited the fort. He remembered Ken because he had asked about a village close to their starting point in the Nebraska Territory that Indians might have raided. No, the officer did not know whether they planned to go to Oregon or California, but he remarked on how they were way behind all of the other trains going west. He said they had two large, covered wagons pulled by oxen and a buckboard pulled by a huge draft horse. They also had other livestock, including several horses, and had passed Fort Laramie only about three or four weeks ago.

We were getting closer. We sat down with the maps in the evening and made a plan. Three hundred and seventy miles lay between Fort Laramie and Fort Bridger. We could easily drive there in one day.

As we drove on toward western Wyoming, things started going wrong. First, it was a flat tire on the travel trailer. We had a spare, but it was also flat.

Sam cursed the company that rented us the trailer. Then, leaving Daddy with the trailer, we drove to the next exit and had the spare tire pumped up and the other one repaired. One day wasted. We only traveled about fifty miles.

The following morning, after spending the night at a small ranch where we could let the horses graze, we discovered the truck would not start. Yet another delay. This time everyone stayed behind except Daddy and Sam, who left to find a new battery. John had examined the vehicle and decided it was the problem. I wasn't so sure. Late in the day, we had the truck towed into the nearest town, only to have a mechanic discover the fuel line had a big cut and the battery was dead. With both fixed, we were back on the road and headed to Fort Bridger. It was the 15th of August.

The country we drove through was spectacular, but I wanted to get to Fort Bridger and find Greg, Ken and Emily, and Mom Nellie and James. I wanted to be there NOW, but with each vehicle pulling a trailer, we had to keep well below the speed limit. Finally, we exited I-80 and drove on past the entrance to the park to a nearby ranch where the STTIU had arranged for us to camp. It was near enough that we could ride the horses to the fort in the morning.

The evening became unbearable. We were so close and yet so far, 163 years too far away. When morning came, I begged and begged to be allowed to go along. I mean, we had four horses, so four people could go. After refusing, then reconsidering (more logic and begging on my part), Daddy let me go along, but he made me promise to keep quiet and follow his instructions completely. So we saddled up at the ranch, rode into a grove of trees, and jumped. Thank heavens for Maisie's abilities. We followed the Little Black Fork of the Green River from the ranch to the fort, about a five minute ride. When it came into sight, I was shocked. Fort Bridger in 1853 was nothing more than some upright logs, with the bark still attached, which formed a stockade of sorts, and a few buildings here and there. The noise from one led me to believe it was a blacksmith shop.

Daddy led us to the trading post. The plan was for Maisie and me to stay with the horses, while he and Sam asked questions. Before we could even enter the trading post, a dark-skinned, Spanish man dressed in buckskin pants and a cream-colored linen shirt came out and introduced himself.

"I am Louis Vasquez, how can I help you? I don't have many supplies right now as most of the settlers have already passed this way. You're not Mormon, are you?"

"No, we're not Mormon. We're looking for friends who started out late on the trail from Nebraska. Their family name is Harrison, Ken Harrison. He is traveling with a Negro family by the name of Jackson. Have they passed this way?"

"No, no, haven't seen anyone at all lately, especially no one traveling with Negroes. Most everyone who passes this way stops in to leave letters for back home or to stock up on needed supplies. Is your train near by?" he asked curiously.

"Oh, no, several miles away. We're camped for a few days hoping to meet up with the Harrison party. We came from Oregon and plan to go to California with them. Perhaps we'll drop by again tomorrow. If the Harrison train comes by, it's only two covered wagons and a buckboard, can you tell them Matthew Engram was here looking for him and we'll stop back by every day or so?"

"Yes, yes, I can do so. Please, don't you need any supplies?"

"Thank you, not today. Much obliged," Daddy replied and off we rode.

I wanted to cry. Maisie reached across and patted my shoulder. Once out of sight of the fort, Daddy and Sam called stop, and we all dismounted.

"Rose, please don't worry. They may have been delayed. We'll check back tomorrow and the next day. Then, if they have not appeared, we'll have to rethink our plans," Daddy said.

That was the 16th. The news on the 17th was the same. No sign of the Harrisons. On the evening of the 17th, John declared the whole mission to be a waste of time. Daddy and Sam tried to change his mind, but it ended in a massive argument. Afterward, each wandered off alone in opposite directions. If it hadn't been for Maisie and Holly, I would have lost my mind with worry and indecision.

On the morning of the 18th, after a lot of thought during the night, I made up my mind. I dressed in my nineteenth-century clothing, packed a knife (I couldn't get to a gun), a topographic map of the area, and some food and water in a pack. I left the trailer before anyone else was awake and was just to the grove of trees, where we had time jumped each day, when Maisie appeared. She had been walking Boone.

"Rose, are ye going somewhere?"

"I'm going to search for the Harrisons. I've got a map and plan to go to Fort Bridger and then up the Oregon Trail toward South Pass. They have to be somewhere between South Pass and here," I reasoned.

"Alone?" Maisie asked with concern.

"Yes, alone. I've been in the past before ALONE and can do it again."

"How about I go with ye, and bring two horses? We could search faster that way."

"Really, you'd do that for me?"

"Aye, but I'm going to leave a note for Holly before we go."

Maisie returned in about five minutes with packed saddle bags and a rifle. We saddled Mattie and Cody and headed out. Boone immediately leapt onto Cody, right behind the saddle.

"I see Boone doesn't wish to be left behind. Maybe he'll come in handy," was Maisie's only comment.

We jumped and rode toward Fort Bridger. Just as we arrived at the fort's gate, so did a scruffy-looking man dressed in buckskin and leading a horse packed with hides and pelts.

"Ladies, you out here alone?" he asked.

"Nay, my husband's coming along. He stopped a wee bit back to get a rock out of his horse's hoof. We've been coming here for several days asking about the Harrison's wagon train. We're trying to meet up with them. Ye wouldn't happen to have seen them, two wagons and a buckboard?" Maisie asked with only a slight hesitation.

"Didn't see no wagons, but met Mr. Harrison up in the mountains above the Sweetwater River. Helped him get his horse back, big black stallion it was, said they were headed to California. Did you ask Louis?"

"Aye. He hasn't seen them."

"Let me leave off this pack horse and ask around some. You ladies wait right here. Fort can be somewhat disreputable early in the morning like this."

So we waited.

Finally, we saw our scruffy friend and Louis approaching.

"This is my partner Jim Bridger. He says he told you he met Mr. Harrison. Since their party has not yet made it here, we think you should ask at the Mormon Ferry on the Green River about twenty-five or so miles north of here," Louis stated.

"Excuse me, sir," I asked. "Did Louis say your name is Jim Bridger? Jim Bridger, the mountain man?"

"Yep, Jim Bridger, mountain man, trapper, and part owner of this goin' concern. You heard of me?"

"Oh, yes sir, from newspapers back east." I responded, quite in awe of the man.

"Well, you ladies don't go no farther without your menfolk. Indian trouble between here and the ferry, and those pesky Mormons are just as bad," he answered. Then, he and Louis walked back into the fort without another backward glance.

"It appears Jim and Louis don't care for Mormons," Maisie remarked.

"Oh, in 1853, Mormon travelers accused them of over pricing goods and selling liquor to the Indians. A few weeks from now, the Mormons will capture the fort and take over the whole business for themselves. Jim and Louis will be driven out. It's a long story, and I don't remember all the details. Bridger probably sold liquor to the Indians. As for over pricing goods, well, he and Louis had to purchase and then ship everything they sold, either from St. Louis or San Francisco, so they had enormous overhead cost," I answered.

On the way back, we met Daddy and Sam, walking, as neither could bring horses to 1853. Daddy was furious with me and threatened to ground me FOREVER. Maisie talked him down and explained what we had learned. We walked back to the camp to find John gone. He'd left a note.

Good Luck with this crazy quest. Going home. Got a ride to the nearest airport. Sam, find a new partner.
John.

"Wonder where he found a ride?" Sam queried. "Oh well, back to our problem. Maisie, let Holly know what's happening, and we'll get going."

Maisie and Holly loaded the horses, with Cody and Mattie still saddled. We had never unhitched the vehicles from the trailers, so we moved out in record time. We left I-80 and drove back north east to a little town called Bryan. From there we took a small road north to the Seedskadee National Wildlife Refuge and the junction of a small road that took us over to where the ferry once crossed, about two miles from the junction. I used my laptop and phone to guide us along. It had taken us almost an hour to drive to the area of Wyoming's Green River ferry.

"Daddy, if you turn left at the next intersection, there's a road with a cutoff and parking area on the right. We should be able to park there and unload the horses."

"Thanks, Rose."

Sam was busy calling the STTIU to give them an update on our progress. He also reported John's decision to return to headquarters.

"Do I understand he didn't inform you of his intentions, or as far as you can tell he didn't book a flight?" Sam asked whomever he was speaking with.

"Okay, keep me informed please," Sam requested, turning toward Daddy.

"Matthew, John never called the Unit to request a flight home. Strange. Oh well, we have better people to worry about right now."

There was only a truck hitched to an empty four-horse trailer at the turnout. We parked, unloaded the horses, and jumped into 1853, leaving Holly in 2016. Within minutes, we could see the wagons.

"Greg, Greg," I shouted excitedly. But it wasn't Greg who answered. It was Mom Nellie.

"Rose, child, how on earth did you get here? How did you find us?" she exclaimed while climbing down from a covered wagon and rushing toward me.

I jumped down and ran toward her. We hugged and hugged while Daddy, Sam, and Maisie dismounted. Maisie took the reins of all four horses and walked over to tie them to the buckboard. Soon, James joined us from the second wagon, and before we could even begin to explain how we found them, he urged Daddy and Sam aside. Still holding Mom Nellie, I realized she was crying.

"Rose, Emily's hurt, and Greg's missing. Oh, thank the good Lord you've come! You don't know how much we've missed you," she stammered through her tears. "You can go back to 2016, can't you, Rose?"

"Yes, Mom Nellie, we can go back, all of us can go back," I whispered, patting her back and hugging her once again. My mind slowly took in Mom Nellie's statement that *Greg was missing*. How could that be, I had come all this way to find him. How could he not be here?

Daddy, Sam, and James joined Mom Nellie and me. James gave me a big hug and filled us in on the first events of the 15th of August including how Emily was hurt.

"How is Emily now?" Maisie asked, wandering over to listen in to the conversation. "I'm a veterinarian, but I'll be happy to check her over."

Mom Nellie gratefully led Maisie to the Harrisons' wagon, while James continued. I wanted to see Emily, but knew James was about to explain how and why Greg was missing.

James continued to explain, "Ken and I arrived soon after hearing the rifle shots. The ferryman and his wife filled us in on what had happened, and about Greg jumping his horse into the river and being pulled down river by the current. By then, Nellie had arrived on the opposite bank. We used the ferry to cross and found Emily still unconscious, with Nellie standing guard over her with a loaded pistol. Only then did we realize Greg was missing,"

I began to shake and silently tears flowed. I knew all this had happened while we wasted time with flat tires and such. I should have worked harder to find them. We should have moved faster.

About that time, Maisie returned looking very concerned, "Sam, we need to get Emily to a hospital. She has a severe concussion and a fever. Can you ride back and tell Holly to arrange for EMS to pick her up at the parking lot? Matthew, can you and James harness the small wagon? She's conscious, but won't be able to ride." Maisie had evaluated the situation and directed everyone like a true professional.

"Matthew, why is she with you? Who exactly is she?" asked James.

"Her name's Maisie. I'll explain later."

"James, I can't go with her," Mom Nellie cried, "Someone needs to go with her, but I can't leave Baidepe."

"Who is Baidepe?" Daddy and I asked together. Then Daddy asked, "James, where's Ken?"

"Baidepe is an Indian girl we found. She's been traveling with us. We've adopted her. Ken's been searching for Greg each day for three days. At Emily's insistence, he goes out each day and returns at dusk. Greg's horse Ghost came back alone about two hours after the accident. We haven't found even as much as a trace of Greg. I'm afraid he drowned. I hunt for him when I can, but after the incident, I can't leave Nellie and Emily alone, so I can only search nearby," James answered.

Things happened quickly then. Daddy and James hitched the big draft horse to the buckboard, emptied most of its contents, and placed a feather tick and several quilts into the wagon bed. James carried Emily to the wagon and tucked her in. While James drove the wagon to where we had left our vehicles, I stayed with Mom Nellie. Daddy later told me how an EMS helicopter arrived about twenty minutes after they got to the parking lot and jumped to 2016. Holly rode with Emily to the hospital while Maisie returned with Daddy and Sam. Sam now had his satellite phone with him and could jump back and check on Emily as needed. Isn't technology great!

Still, throughout all this, I could hear Nellie and James telling us about how Greg was still missing and possibly drowned in that rushing river I could see so clearly from their camp. My heart kept saying, "I can't lose Greg, I just can't." So, I decided right there and then that he was not dead. Yet, my mind forgot to tell my eyes and my heart, so my tears kept flowing and my heart felt like it was breaking.

19
Looking for Greg

Without explaining how and why to everyone, we all agreed our time would be better spent looking for Greg. I would not believe he was dead. *No, not happening*, as he would say.

Daddy and Sam wanted to move the wagons to the cutoff where our vehicles were parked, but then Ken would not know where James and Nellie had gone. We all seemed to forget that Ken didn't even know we had come to their rescue. We settled on a plan. Sam and Maisie would stay with the wagons, get everything ready to move out, and wait for our return. In the meantime, James, Daddy, and I would search for Greg and Ken.

We split up. James and I took the ferry across the Green River and rode off downstream. James passed me one of their extra rifles right before we boarded the ferry. He stuck a Colt pistol into a conveniently placed holster on his saddle. Daddy had a modern pistol Sam had given him. We also had handheld portable radios, so we could communicate. James and I rode downstream, watching the bank for his body, and calling Greg's name over and over. Otherwise, we didn't talk much. About two hours later, we came to a second ferry crossing.

"Rose, this is the Robinsons' ferry. Stay here and let me ask about Greg."

I waited and watched as James approached the ferryman. They talked for only a few minutes before James reported back.

"He says another man passed here about an hour or so ago. I think it must have been Ken, although I thought he was on the other side of the river. Let's keep going."

Once out of sight, using the radio, we checked in with Daddy. He'd also had no luck. Then Sam called and told us Emily was still being evaluated and was very agitated about Greg. Holly decided to stay with her. Another hour of searching and now several miles down river, James and I stopped to eat the sandwiches Holly had packed that morning. We had just remounted when I motioned for James to listen. I'd become aware of voices, human voices, coming from downstream. James and I rode toward the sound, dismounted, and crept forward, trying to use the trees for cover. Not being able to hear clearly what was being said, we didn't know if they were Indians or white settlers.

Before we could determine who was talking, we caught the sounds of them riding off. It took several minutes for us to get back to our horses and go after them. By late afternoon, we had still not caught up with whomever we were following or found Greg. We were now out of radio range of the camp and could only contact Daddy. Just when we decided to turn back, a rifle shot and a shout rang out. We spurred our horses toward the sound. As we rode into a small clearing, James and I saw a man raise his rifle and aim across the river toward a man on horseback.

Just before he fired, the man with the rifle yelled, "Damn you, Ken Harrison!"

Without thinking, I had grabbed my rifle, cocked it, steadied my aim, just as Annie Oakley had taught me, and fired. I didn't shoot high this time. Nope, I hit the man with the rifle square in the shoulder, and he fell like a rock. Meanwhile, James pulled his pistol, dismounted, and ran toward the bank. Across the river, I could see Ken emerge from the other side of a solid black horse, holding his rifle steadily aimed toward us.

"James, is that you?"

"Yeah, you hit?"

"Just a flesh wound. Who'd you shoot?" Ken shouted.

"Not me, Rose shot him."

"Rose?"

"Yeah, Rose. I'll explain later. River's too high for you to cross safely. Matthew should be somewhere on your side looking for you and Greg. Stay there. I'll call him on the radio."

"What radio?"

Now, I'd never shot anyone before, but I'd decided in that instance, I couldn't let this man shoot Greg's dad. I didn't feel bad at all for taking the shot, I knew right then the guilt would arrive later. When I dismounted and moved toward the man I'd shot, who now lay moaning on the ground, James handed me the man's rifle. I looked down and gasped, "John Bomgarten? I shot John?"

"Rose, do you know this man?"

Still shocked, I took a moment before answering. "Yes, he's a STTIU agent that's been helping us. But this morning, he left to go back to headquarters. Said he thought we were on a wild goose chase," I answered shakily.

"Rose, Maisie put a small first aid kit in my saddlebag. There's also an extra shirt. Bring over both."

I fetched the supplies while James called Daddy on the radio and told him what had happened. Daddy agreed to jump back and call for help. We used the shirt and gauze pads in the kit to staunch the bleeding. Then, using the coin in my bracelet, James and I jumped back to 2016 with John. We waited until yet another helicopter circled overhead and landed to pick up John. He was unconscious by this time, probably in shock from the loss of blood.

"Hey," the emergency medical services technician said, "this is the second time today, we've had to pick up someone dressed like you. You shooting a movie or something?"

"Yeah," I answered, wondering how to explain who shot John.

"Who shot him? Did someone forget and use live ammunition?" the tech asked.

"No idea, shot came out of nowhere. Must have been a hunter. I thought we were safe here in a wildlife refuge. We'll meet you at the hospital after we report this to the police," James answered, thinking quickly.

"Sure," shouted the tech, as they loaded John into the copter.

As soon as it was out of sight, James and I jumped back. Daddy was now beside Ken, on the other side of the river, helping him bandage his upper arm.

"Rose, are you okay?" Daddy shouted.

"I think so. I shot John. He shot Ken. What's going on, Daddy? Why was John here trying to kill Ken? I thought he was helping us? Do you think he did something to Greg? Does he know where Greg is?"

"I don't know, Rose, I just don't know, but we'll get to the bottom of all this soon enough," Daddy assured me. "We'll meet you back at the Robinsons' ferry," Daddy shouted one more time as he and Ken turned back toward the ferries and their camp.

In 1853, James and I rode back to the Robinsons' ferry, leading John's horse. Along the way we spent time looking for any sign of Greg. Almost at dusk, we crossed over and met up with Ken and Daddy. Back at the camp, we explained all that had happened to Sam, Maisie, and Nellie. After moving the wagons to the parking lot area, Sam escorted Ken back to 2016 and drove him to see Emily at the hospital in Evanston, some 60 or so miles away. Sam also planned to call the Unit, report what had happened, and ask for backup.

I helped Maisie and Nellie make supper. Maisie and I talked about how we might find Greg and how we could ask the STTIU for help. I couldn't keep my thoughts on what I was doing instead of how to find Greg. We needed better maps, like the ones I had left in the truck.

Later, Maisie jumped back to our time to retrieve Boone, and she brought along some *modern* food. Boone and Becky made friends. Boone's superior herding skills kept the puppy out of trouble for the rest of the evening. Maisie had also had called Sam and asked him to bring my maps to us when he returned.

Only when we were ready to eat did Nellie go to their wagon and urge Baidepe to join us. She'd been hiding most of the day. Once she came out, Nellie introduced her to each of us. Baidepe whispered back our names and then climbed into James' lap. I remembered doing the same many years ago. She was small and thin, but clean and well groomed. She knew quite a bit of English and conversed with James and Nellie, but refused to speak with me or Maisie.

After our improvised meal, Maisie once again jumped back and returned with a carton of vanilla ice cream and the remains of an apple pie. We laughed at Baidepe's expression after tasting her first bite of the frozen concoction. She ate from everyone's bowl and began talking to us. Maisie seemed to be her favorite. She touched Maisie's hair over and over again. I guess, she had never seen someone with red hair. My own long hair, now barely braided after a long day of riding, is dark like Baidepe's.

With us all sitting around the campfire, James and Nellie related much of what had occurred when they were kidnapped, and of their trip along the Oregon Trail. I was so jealous of their adventure until I remembered Greg was missing and had been so for almost three days. Daddy and I explained the events of the last few months, including our search along the trail and how Jim Bridger had suggested we come to the ferry and ask about them.

Several hours after dark, exhaustion overtook us all. James, Nellie, and Baidepe returned to their wagon to sleep. I bedded down in the Harrisons' wagon, and Daddy took the first watch. We had re-circled the wagons and gathered up all the livestock. Maisie returned to our time and planned to sleep there in case Ken or Sam needed to get in touch with us. As I snuggled in, I remembered how James and I'd heard *voices*, as in two or more people speaking. Not just John. Had we been mistaken? No, I didn't think so. I decided to tell Daddy in the morning. I was just too tired now to climb back out of the wagon. So, I said my prayers, putting in one last plea for Greg to be safe. All evening he had been ever present in my thoughts.

20
Fort Bridger

I awoke to the sound of Ken's voice.

"Nellie, she insisted I come back and search for Greg. She's stable. The doctor says she has a severe concussion and is dehydrated. They have her on fluids. They did an ultrasound, and said the baby is fine. They want to keep her for at least another day. When they release her, I want her to go home. I think you and Rose should go too. James and I can stay here and search for Greg. I have to know. . . I have to know one way or the other," Ken stated, his voice breaking with emotion.

It was James who answered. "Ken, Nellie and I can't go home to our time. We discussed it with Maisie last night. Maisie and I tried, but Baidepe can't time travel, and as you may know, Maisie can't take her along. It doesn't work with humans. If they don't have the DNA gene, humans just can't time travel. Nellie and I've discussed it. We're going on to California to live, in this time."

"James, Nellie, you can't," Daddy pleaded.

"Yes, we can, Matthew. And we're going to," Nellie confirmed. "James and I have been talking about it since we found Baidepe. We've always wanted children of our own, and now God has provided us with a daughter. She depends on us, and we love her. We could never imagine giving her up. We'll still be able to visit. You can come back and see us. Or we'll come there, one at a time, and see you and Rose. We can't desert Rose. We still love her as much as we always have. We'd like for her to visit us from time to time and get to know her new sister," Nellie explained.

"Sounds like a plan to me," I said, climbing down from the Harrisons' wagon. "But today, I suggest we move the wagons south toward Fort Bridger and search for Greg along the way. Ken do you have my maps? It occurred to me that since we drove up here to the ferry instead of taking the trail in 1853, we might have missed some travelers whom we could have asked. Also, if you're going to California, you're awfully late to go through the Sierra Nevadas. You're going to hit snow. What's more important is James and I overheard at least two men talking a while before we came upon John shooting Ken. Any ideas as to whom he was speaking?" I finished with a flurry.

"Yep, she's still in charge of the world," answered Sam.

"Oh, and one more thing," I asked quietly. "Is John alive? Did he say anything about why?"

"Rose, John is alive. His shoulder is a mess, and he lost a lot of blood, but he'll likely survive. STTIU agents are on hand and are holding him for questioning. He'll need surgery soon. Everyone is really proud of your skill and willingness to save Ken's life. We figure John's been working with the Pirate's gang all along," Sam answered. "I think he tried to delay us by cutting the fuel line and flattening those two tires. What surprises me is his willingness to kill Ken. I guess we won't know more until he's questioned."

Once again, we started making plans. Nellie, James, Maisie, and I would move the wagons south along the trail. It was about twenty-five miles to Fort Bridger. Daddy and Ken would search for Greg. Sam jumped back to drive one of our modern vehicles, while Holly would drive the other. To make things easier for us, they would take our four ranch horses in the van.

Before we could move out, Maisie and I got lessons from James and Nellie on how to hitch the oxen and Budweiser. Maisie also got a lesson on driving oxen, while I learned how to drive the buckboard. James would ride Ghost and scout the trail and keep the cattle herded. Daddy rode Clown, and Ken rode Midnight. Once again, they headed out in search of Greg.

Just before we moved out, I pulled Ken aside. "Is Emily truly going to have a baby? Does Greg know?" I asked.

"Oh, Rose, yes, Greg knows. He didn't take the news too well to begin with. Turns out it was more worry about his Mom than being mad about a baby. Also, we didn't tell him right off. You will be surprised when we find him. He's grown so much, and I don't mean taller. He's handled situations like an adult." And with that, he gave me a big hug and mounted up.

"Help us think of a name. It's a girl," he called as he joined Daddy. I knew he was only trying to take my mind off Greg's situation.

That area of what is now Wyoming is spectacular. First, we proceeded across a high plains area, dry and full of sage and snakes. A warm breeze blew almost all day, sometimes stronger and filled with grainy bits that stung your skin. By midday, we had moved into a pass between mountains in the distance and large buttes closer by. I could see antelope and once thought I saw mountain goats. I could smell sage and cedar almost constantly. The area stayed dry, and every stream we passed had long ago dried up. At some points, we could see for miles and miles, and at others, barely around the next bend or gap in the landscape. Late in the day, we saw Church Buttes, a large sandstone formation. In another five miles or so, we arrived in an area with a large rock overhang. A small stream nearby had only enough water for some of our stock. We used our barrels to water the rest. We circled our wagons, and Nellie and I began preparing a meal. Maisie jumped back and reported our location to Holly. She and Sam had returned to the ranch where we had camped earlier in the week. They planned to drive into Evanston to check on Emily. Sam was hoping to arrange for Holly to remain with her at the hospital.

"Nellie, I should have gone out on horseback to search with Ken and Daddy. I think tomorrow I'll go along," I whispered. I had worried all day.

"Greg, my brother, he strong. He come home," stated Baidepe firmly. The first words she'd uttered all day.

Baidepe proved to be quite a helpmate to Nellie. She gathered sage to burn, stirred the pot, carried water, and even used her slingshot to bring down a desert cottontail. It didn't surprise me much when she also gutted and cleaned it, carefully saving the hide. So we added roasted rabbit to our evening meal.

Maisie checked all the animals while we cooked. She treated the oxen's feet and declared Ghost to be expecting. James puttered about putting everything in its place, often glancing about for Daddy and Ken. It was dark when they caught up with us. Ken immediately jumped back to 2016 to call Emily and give her an update.

"Daddy, is Ken okay? Did you even see any sign of Greg?" I asked.

"Nothing. Ken's about brokenhearted. He blames himself for letting Greg take the wagons forward to the ferry. He said he only did so because he expected a raid on the livestock, after seeing Indian signs for several days. He figured they were out to steal another horse or cow."

"From what Nellie and James have told us, it sounds like Greg had been pulling his own weight and acting all grown up for a month or so. Ken told me the same thing. Is there anything we can do to help?" I asked, giving Daddy a big hug.

"Oh, Sam's working on getting a search and rescue team here from headquarters to help. We hope they'll be here tomorrow. It took a while to find enough TTIs with the right kind of training," he replied. I could hear doubt in his voice.

After dinner, we bedded down once again. Maisie and I slept in the Harrisons' wagon, while Daddy and Ken camped underneath in bedrolls. I could hear them talking softly late into the night. The following morning, Ken announced how he was abandoning the search along the river and planned to go into Fort Bridger and ask Jim for help. We started out early, and by nine o'clock (I had my wristwatch in my pocket), we approached the fort.

Daddy suggested we wait outside while Ken and James asked to see Jim. As they left our camp, Boone escaped from where we had tied him and dashed past them into the fort. Ken shouted for him to stay as they ran after him.

The Black Fork, which ran alongside the fort, had a good stream of fresh water, so Maisie and I took the livestock on down. Daddy was preparing to fill our buckets and barrels when I became aware of two riders approaching. I turned just in time to see the couple clearly as they approached. At the fort's gate, the man dismounted and entered while the woman grabbed his horse's reins and rode down toward the stream. I moved behind Spook and motioned for Maisie to join me, but she couldn't see me from where she was standing. I couldn't very well yell out, so I did the next best thing.

I pulled my pistol (I'd borrowed it from James that morning) and moved cautiously closer and closer to the woman while she watered their horses. When I felt I was close enough, I said calmly, "Keep your right hand on the reins, but use your left to drop the pistol on your hip into the stream. I've already shot John and won't hesitate to shoot you as well." I had recognized her right off, no matter how she was dressed. This was the Pirate's partner who had followed me from Denver to New York, and the man who had entered the fort, was none other than the Pirate.

Luckily for me, she followed my instructions. Since my insides were shaking and I wanted to vomit, I really didn't know if I could shoot someone else. Maisie called for Daddy, and before I knew it, there he was. Maisie took the reins from the woman's grasp while Daddy escorted her back toward our wagons.

"Daddy, she can time travel. Don't let go!" I called out.

"Nellie, find me some rope," he urged, as we got closer to the wagons. Maisie helped Nellie tie the woman's hands, but knowing she could still time jump, someone had to keep a hand on her.

"Daddy, the Pirate's in the fort with Ken and James."

"Okay, Rose, breathe. I'll deal with that. You stay here and don't let go of her. Keep your pistol pointed right at her."

Daddy ran toward the fort, but had not yet reached the gate when a shot rang out. One shot, only one.

Nellie and Maisie ran after him. There I stood, stuck holding a pistol on a woman who had caused my best friend to probably be dead. Then, out of nowhere, a rock flew through the air and hit the woman in the head. Down she went in a heap of skirts. I turned to see Baidepe grinning from ear to ear.

"Good shot," she declared and clapped for herself. I had to laugh. When I was growing up, James and Nellie had always rewarded my achievements by clapping for me.

I sat down next to the fire and pulled Baidepe into my lap. I placed the two pistols, James' and the one from the now unconscious woman, within reach. I really no longer needed either one as our *guest* was out cold. I guess rocks are the enemy of the Pirate and his partner, but this time I wasn't responsible.

Soon I heard Maisie calling my name. "Rose, Rose, look!" And as I turned, the most wonderful sight of all appeared—Ken supporting, almost carrying, a weak, haggard-looking Greg. Boone ran circles around them all and then began barking and jumping on Greg and Ken over and over again.

Behind them, a very serious-looking Jim Bridger held a rifle on the Pirate, while Daddy and James dragged him toward our wagons. I knew if they let go, the Pirate could time jump. I was surprised his partner had not done so before we laid a hand on her. I guess she wasn't willing to leave without him. Upon closer inspection, I could see blood on the Pirate's temple and that he was unconscious.

"Who shot him?" I asked.

"I shot the cur-dog desperado. Don't no one shoot my friends, especially in the back," replied Jim Bridger. "Don't know why Mr. Harrison wants him. If you leave him here, I'll let him rot." With that statement, he turned and walked back toward the fort. That's the last time I ever saw Jim Bridger. Later I read more about all the trouble that would come his way after we left. I felt sorry for him. He had been a true friend to us.

Maisie immediately stepped up, took James' pistol, and moved with Daddy and the Pirate behind the wagons and out of sight.

I rushed to help Ken and James. We placed Greg on a blanket beside the fire. Boone barked and proceeded to lick Greg's face and hands. Baidepe tried to bring Greg a cup of coffee, but Boone spilled it in his lap. So instead she just curled up next to him on the blanket. Ken kept hugging him, and James had tears in his eyes. Nellie stood nearby and sobbed into a large bandana.

Until now, Greg had not said a word. I was crying tears of relief and tears of joy all at the same time. As I collapsed down beside him to give him a hug, he looked up, smiled and winked, and said, "I'm not dead yet."

Becky's constant barking and pulling against her rope brought us all back to the present. James roughly hauled the Pirate's accomplice behind the wagon. He didn't seem to feel the need to be gentle. Then, Maisie and Daddy jumped the Pirate and his friend back to 2016 and called in backup to have them arrested. I didn't care what happened to either of them. I retrieved Becky and brought her over to Greg, while James and Ken decided what to do next.

"Rose, how's my mom? How did you find us? Who's the woman with the red hair? She's pretty. Did you meet Jim Bridger? How did Boone get here? Can you time jump with animals now? Where are we?"

The Greg I knew and loved was back! Nonstop talking and nonstop questions.

"Okay, I'll try to answer them all. First Emily is fine. She's in a nearby hospital for observation and fluids. Oh, it's a girl. Ken told me. We found you by following a lot of clues and with a lot of luck. I'll explain later. The pretty woman with the red hair is Maisie Stuart. She's a twin, a veterinarian, and can time jump with animals. Her sister Holly is here, in 2016, as well. Oh, and we're at Fort Bridger, Wyoming, and yes, I met him, Jim Bridger. Does that answer everything?"

"So, we can go home?" he asked.

I figured I'd better tell him the truth. "All of us, except Baidepe," I answered, "but we can talk about it later."

**Church Buttes, near Fort Bridger,
Wyoming Territory,
photographed in 1868 by
Andrew J. Russell**

21
Back on the Trail

Ken insisted Greg be taken to the hospital in Evanston to be checked out and to see Emily. Off they jumped to 2016, where Greg got to meet Holly and Sam. Daddy and I agreed to stay with James and Nellie, at least for the time being. After all those years when James and Nellie cared for me when Daddy was home and when he was absent, we both knew we owed them. I knew the real reason was love. Daddy and James had become like brothers over the last eleven years. Nellie and James had joined our family right after my Mama died.

Maisie had a hard time deciding what to do. Finally, with Greg admitted to the hospital for antibiotics and fluids, she decided to stay with us to help with the animals. Backup arrived from headquarters to help Sam. They retrieved the red pickup and horse trailer from the cutoff at the ferry after finding out it belonged to the Pirate. Since Ghost was expecting a foal, we replaced her with the bay gelding John had been riding and named him *Traitor*. Poor choice, as he behaved like a dream and had an even, steady gait. The Pirate and his female accomplice had left behind two additional horses, a beautiful gray and white Appaloosa mare I named *Fancy,* and a scruffy looking dun-colored gelding we aptly named *Bridger.* We kept both of these and sent back Midnight. We could return him to James after they got settled. Maisie gave Clown a complete checkup and declared the mare would be fine after some additional grain and vitamins. We also kept Cody and Romeo, but over my objections, Mattie and Little Blackie were returned to the ranch.

The STTIU came through with supplies galore. They brought foodstuffs, grain for the animals, fresh blankets and bedrolls (including some cleverly disguised arctic-weather sleeping bags), clothing, and medical supplies. Nellie gave them Baidepe's clothing sizes, and they furnished her with all sorts of beautiful mid-nineteenth century clothing, much of which she refused to wear. Like most girls, the one dress she liked was pink calico with darker pink flowers.

We had moved to a secluded point where we felt comfortable jumping from time to time. It took Baidepe a while to get used to the appearances and disappearances of various people, but she soon took it in stride, except for constantly asking about Greg, Ken, and Emily.

A week passed. Holly flew back to New York, having declared she loved every minute of our adventure. She promised she would visit us in North Dakota sometime soon. Maisie contacted her practice in Scotland and took an extended leave of absence.

Then on the 25th, Ken and Greg returned with Sam. Ken had persuaded Emily to go home and rest up for at least a week. She took Becky with her and declared she would be housebroken soon. Boone stayed with us. Here we were almost at the end of August, and we still didn't have a plan to get the Jacksons across the mountains and to safety before snow fell in the Sierra Nevadas.

Despite having captured the Pirate and his two accomplices, the STTIU and Ken demanded Emily have protection at the ranch and at her dig site since the size of the Pirate's gang had not yet been determined. Headquarters sent three agents; two men, one of which Emily said was a great cook, and one woman. One man and the woman accompanied Emily to her dig site each day.

Greg looked much better. He was thin and tanned, with even a scruff of a beard. His voice had changed, and he sounded so much like Ken now, I was startled every time he spoke. He looked muscular and acted so grown up.

Sam worked with headquarters, and using some logistical input from Daddy, they created a plan. Maisie jumped back and retrieved eight fresh oxen. The other seven got to go back to the ranch in North Dakota to rest. That evening we held a camp meeting. If Daddy, Maisie, and I all stayed, the camp would be really full. On the other hand, we would have more hands to complete the work. Headquarters loaned us an additional man, named Jesse, to help out. Only about twenty-five, with surfer boy looks, Jesse was back-country survival trained, strong, and a great cook. I think he saw this as an adventure of a lifetime. I later found out Ken had been training him as an assistant. Just between you and me, I loved having him along.

Maisie and I would sleep in the Harrisons' wagon, while the men slept in bedrolls. A satellite phone, hidden in the Harrisons' wagon, would keep us in touch with the modern world and especially Emily. She only agreed to return to the ranch if Ken reported in each night. He and Greg took turns doing so.

The first day back on the Oregon Trail, Daddy let me ride alongside Greg so we could talk. I rode Fancy, and he, of course, rode Cody, with Boone comfortably sitting just behind him on Cody's rump most of the day. We filled each other in on all our time apart. Greg told me about how he got Becky, crossing all the various rivers, Ken's adventure while searching for Midnight, and all the humdrum stuff of the trail. I told him about Annie Oakley, searching for clues, and our trip to the Nebraska airport to begin our time search. That's when I remembered finding his leather bracelet.

"Here, I found this in the hangar at the airport. I thought you might like to have it back," I said, handing it over.

"The Pirate took this. He must have dropped it. Thanks, I've been missing it."

"We also found a coin from 1853 during our search. Is it what the Pirate used to make you jump?"

"Yeah, later we all looked for it. None of us could remember what happened to it after he forced us to jump. Dad figured we must have just dropped it," Greg answered. "Do you still have it?"

"Sure, it's back at the wagons; I'll give it to you tonight." I hesitated and then asked, "Greg, what happened to you at the ferry?"

"Well, first I heard Mom's scream. The ferry with the Jacksons' wagon had already pulled away from the shore. I looked over to see three or four men surrounding our wagon. One of them jumped in right as Mom reached for the pistol, which was hidden behind the seat. It was a Walter Colt. James said it was too valuable to be carried all day in a saddle holster. The man in the wagon pulled it from her hands, hit her upside the head with it, and she collapsed.

"I remember jumping Ghost into the river, and then being pulled farther and farther downstream by the heavy current and undertow. At some point, I knew Ghost and I would both drown if we stayed together, so I grabbed an overhanging branch and let her go. I couldn't hold on for long. Letting go of that branch is really the last thing I remember."

"How did you end up at Fort Bridger?" I whispered, scared to know the answer.

"I don't know. Louis said some Shoshone warriors arrived with me draped across a bay gelding that had thrown a shoe. They wanted the other three horseshoes removed and to purchase ammunition. The fort's blacksmith agreed to do so, but only if they left me behind. Louis said they unceremoniously dumped me off the horse and rode away after getting what they came for. The blacksmith carried me to his quarters, where his American Indian wife took care of me. I remember waking up and being very hot and sick. I slept most of each day and was sleeping when Boone came bounding into their cabin, barking and then growling at the woman. Then Dad and James arrived. And then the Pirate. I felt so weak, and with Boone standing on top of me growling, I didn't manage to say anything before the shot rang out, and the Pirate collapsed, blood gushing from the side of his head. I could see he was only grazed by the shot. I guess if you hadn't brought Boone, Dad might never have found me."

"Sure, he would have. Emily wouldn't let Ken give up. We were there that day to ask Jim Bridger to help us search. Besides, did you think I'd ever give up trying to find you when I'd already come all this way? Silly boy."

"Hey, go back, you said you met Annie Oakley?"

"Yes, Daddy and I flew to Rochester, New York, and saw one of the first shows where Sitting Bull and Annie Oakley both performed in Buffalo Bill's Wild West. Daddy pretended to be a St. Louis newspaper reporter, and we interviewed Annie Oakley. Then she gave me a shooting lesson and taught me how to aim properly. She was magnificent. We watched the show and saw her whole act. We'll have to go sometime. The whole thing, Buffalo Bill, Sitting Bull, amazing."

"Oh, so that's why you didn't shoot high when you shot that man John," he teased.

We moved northwest from Fort Bridger, making good time with fresh oxen and fresh horses. In a little over two days, we passed Fossil Butte, and then on into the mountains, up hills and down gullies, climbing higher and higher each day. One especially steep hill required us to use all eight oxen to pull the first wagon, and then to take them back down the hill to pull up the second wagon. We avoided bad water by having some delivered every few days when possible. At least, it prevented some of the sickness the real pioneers experienced in this area.

The local natives were often barely clothed and starving. Eastbound travelers had warned us they would beg for food. We did what we could. Baidepe continued to hide in the Jacksons' wagon when any native peoples approached.

The trail followed the Bear River, and each evening the temperatures fell. We often took to wearing our winter clothing with long johns underneath. Cedars and willows along the river provided us with plenty of wood, and we stocked up, placing it in the buckboard for those coming days when none could be found or more would be needed. After Soda Springs, we traveled on into today's Idaho toward Fort Hall. The approximately 210 miles from Fort Bridger to Fort Hall took us ten days. Nathaniel J. Wyeth established an early adobe trading fort or post there on the Snake River in 1834. At first Wyeth traded in furs, but by 1853, the fort carried all sorts of goods for those headed to Oregon and California. In 1855, the fort closed after the Ward massacre near Boise, Idaho, and tensions between the immigrants and the Native Americans made it difficult to keep the trading post open.

Today, the fort's archaeological site is located on the Shoshone-Bannock Reservation. Being part Shoshone on my mother's side, I could ask permission to visit the site if I ever wanted to. In 1853, Greg and I purchased horehound candy and new hats for each of us.

Fort Hall lies directly on the Snake River in a beautiful valley that stretches north all the way to the Grand Tetons and Yellowstone. Once out of sight of the post, we moved on south, still following the river. We passed American Falls and then approached a narrow gorge in the rocks, so narrow only one wagon could pass through at a time. In 1853, it was known as Devil's Gate. Some nine years later, Devil's Gate was the site of several minor massacres. Later immigrants renamed it *Massacre Rock* to commemorate the 1862 events where ten pioneers lost their lives.

At last we arrived at the parting of the trails—one followed the Snake River on to Oregon, and our choice, the California Trail, followed southwest along the Raft River some sixty-five miles to the City of Rocks. I Googled it when we got back and it is now a national park. City of Rocks has these granite spires and bluffs, they look kind of like a city made out of rock. The weather had turned cooler as winter approached, and Greg and I spent that evening riding between the formations and wishing we had time to climb a few.

One quiet evening Greg and I were talking when Baidepe came over to Greg and asked bluntly, "Emily dead?"

"No Baidepe, she went home, to our home," he answered. Then turning to me, "Rose, how do I explain this to her?"

"Baidepe, remember when we found Greg at Fort Bridger?"

"Yes, Jim Bridger had my brother."

"Okay. Remember how Maisie and Sam and Jesse just appeared out of the air?" I asked.

"White man magic. White men have magic to disappear, to come and go," she said waving her hands about.

"No, Baidepe. Not all white men can disappear," Greg answered. "Look." Then, taking hold of his bracelet, Greg popped into 2016 and then returned about five seconds later. "Wow, scary highway," he shouted.

"What highway? Greg, Rose, what are you two up to? Answer me right now."

"Nellie, it's okay. Baidepe was asking about Emily. She thinks she's dead. We were just trying to explain about her being at the ranch when the subject of us appearing and disappearing came up. So, Greg demonstrated."

"Yeah, stupid thing to do. I found myself in the middle of a highway with a tractor trailer bearing down on me." For a minute, he sounded like the teenager I once knew back in North Dakota.

"Greg Harrison, what were you thinking pulling a stunt like that? What would I tell Emily if something happened to you again? She wanted you home instead of finishing this trip. She is worried to death every single day. It's not good for her with the baby coming. I declare, I'll tie you up in a wagon if you ever do anything of the sort again."

I think Nellie would have continued if James and Ken had not arrived. Hushing her, James quietly picked her up in his arms and carried her off. In a little while I could hear her sobbing, something I knew she rarely did. I felt so ashamed.

Later, Greg and I apologized and promised not to time travel except when Greg popped out to call his Mom. Maisie sat down and talked with Baidepe. Afterward, Baidepe would tell Greg at least once each day, "Emily go home. She come back, someday, bring baby."

Finally, at Granite Pass, we crossed into Utah and then rather quickly into today's Nevada and moved southwest toward the Great Humboldt River Basin. This portion of the trail passed numerous springs that gave us fresh water. Maisie and I often washed our hair in spring water in the evenings. Before long Baidepe came to join us. She loved shampoo! We taught her to blow bubbles. She even let us put ribbons in her hair.

Lying in the rain shadow of the Sierra Nevada Mountains, the Great Humboldt River Basin consists of a dry, hot, and rough desert, except for the areas directly adjacent to the Humboldt River, which flows nearly due west. Easy to follow, the early pioneers, headed to California, found the water to be good with great fishing when they first reached the Humboldt. James and Nellie both loved to fish and provided our evening meals for several days, but Jesse proved himself to be the best fisherman by landing the largest fish three days in a row.

Wood remained scarce, and we gathered all we could from the occasional junipers and willows. We still depended heavily on sagebrush, as we saved our store of wood in the buckboard for emergencies. The thing almost totally lacking was grass. Thank heavens, we had stocked up on grain for our livestock. Day after day we traveled west across this great desert. The water got muddier and more smelly with each day's travel. After progressing about sixty-five miles along the Humboldt, we encountered the five-mile long narrow Carlin Canyon. Here, the meandering Humboldt passed through a steep mountain gorge, where the river valley narrowed to the width of the stream bed in places. We crossed over the Humboldt some five times before we left the canyon walls behind.

At the first crossing, both Greg and Ken looked nervous. Maisie politely urged Budweiser into the stream and crossed without a problem. She didn't say anything, just motioned me over. I was driving the Harrisons' wagon and urged their oxen forward. I saw Greg ride Cody up next to the Harrisons' lead ox and drive him on across. After that crossing, the Humboldt brought us no great anxiety. Of course, the river was very low in mid-September.

West of Carlin Canyon, we climbed through Emigrant Pass, away from the Humboldt and descended to rejoin the river at Gravelly Ford. As its name indicates, Gravelly Ford had a nice even gravel bottom. Jesse rode ahead and returned with news of a fresh water spring and plenty of grass on the other side of the now very muddy river. Using twentieth-century maps, we realized the trail split at this point, one on both the north and south banks of the river. The two trails reunite at the Humboldt Sink. So, after taking a day of rest, we crossed back at the ford and followed the northern trail.

Three hundred miles from where the California Trail joined the river, the Humboldt disappears into the desert sand. We'd reached the Humboldt first on the 11th of September and traveled fifteen days along it until it disappeared. We marked the calendar on the 26th of September, when the Humboldt was no more. We knew the worst was yet to come.

"... forty memorable miles of bottomless sand, into which the coach wheels sunk from six inches to a foot. We worked our passage most of the way across. That is to say, we got out and walked. It was a dreary pull and a long and thirsty one, for we had no water. From one extremity of this desert to the other, the road was white with the bones of oxen and horses. It would hardly be an exaggeration to say that we could have walked the forty miles and set our feet on a bone at every step! The desert was one prodigious graveyard. And the log chains, wagon tires, and rotting wrecks of vehicles were almost as thick as the bones. "

Mark Twain in *Roughing It.*

22
Crossing the Forty Mile Desert

Forty miles of real desert. No water, no grass, only sand and heat. Both guidebooks and my maps all said we next had to cross some forty miles of pure tortuous desert. The books suggested the trip was best done at night. We arrived at the end of the Humboldt River on the 26th of September. The moon was a waning crescent. In days, we would have no moonlight at all. We could not wait until the ninth of October for the first quarter moon, or even later for a full moon. We needed to cross immediately, in the dead of night, trying to make at least twenty to twenty-five miles before the next sunrise, so that after the second night we would reach water. We rested the following day, and the one after, September 28th. That day, Ken called Emily, and the STTIU delivered several collapsible bladders of water.

By crossing the Forty Mile Desert, a barren stretch of alkali wasteland, we would reach the Carson River, and our chosen trail across the Sierra Nevada Mountains. Two trails led across this desert, which covered an area of over 70 by 150 miles of loose, white, salt-covered sands and baked alkali clay.

Both reflected the sun's heat onto daytime travelers and their livestock. Rain rarely fell in this desert, and we couldn't even hope to see rain at this point in autumn, the hottest and driest time of the year. I had read an article while researching the trail back before we even left North Dakota. It said, in 1850, the Forty Mile Desert accounted for 1,061 dead mules, about 5,000 dead horses, 3,750 dead cattle and oxen, and 953 emigrant graves. We were all a bit worried, but at least we were prepared.

We left our camp at about seven in the evening of the 28th. We had all discussed it and figured this would give us a head start. Immediately, we noticed the deep dust settling on everything. We tied bandanas around our noses. Nellie and Maisie tried to cover everything in the wagons, while Daddy and Greg covered the buckboard with its now hole-ridden cover. In order to go as many miles as possible during the first night, we all rode, either in wagons or on horseback, for the first part of the evening. Each of us had a canteen, our ration of water for the night.

Several hours after dark, Ken called a halt. We watered all of the horses, cows, oxen, and Boone. Nellie checked on the chickens. She had moved their cages inside the buckboard, and each was roosting quietly. Then we walked for about three hours. I was so tired and oh so cold. Late September days may be hot in the desert, but nighttime temperatures plummet to the low thirties, or below. Nellie and Maisie had provided us all with gloves or mittens, heavy coats, sweaters for underneath, hats, and scarves. What I didn't have was decent warm boots! Or even good socks. Soon I felt as if I was walking on ice cubes. Ice cubes covered in sand—for the fine-grained, white sand covered everything.

All night we trudged over hard-packed roads, followed by deep sand, then rough rocks, then sand, then rocks . . .. At dawn, my time came to ride in the wagon. I collapsed beside Baidepe, just as the sun hinted at the coming day. The others walked. No one rode except Maisie and me in the Harrisons' wagon and Nellie and Baidepe in their wagon. Greg and Jesse switched off in the buckboard. Daddy planned to let me sleep for several hours. I awoke to find myself covered in sweat and began stripping out of my heavy clothing. When I stumbled from the wagon, I found most of the others asleep under them, and our livestock standing crowded in the sparse shade provided by the wagons. Budweiser alone stood in the sun, asleep, his head hanging down with his nose almost touching the ground. Not knowing if horses could sunburn, and him being light gray, I threw an old blanket over him. The sun rose higher, and the temperature rose significantly. Soon, we had all stripped down to little more than decent coverings.

Nellie awoke, made tea with honey, and passed it about in tin cups almost too hot to hold. She didn't even have to heat the water. At her urging, we all ate leftover biscuits with honey and butter, both of which ran off the biscuits and down our arms. Jesse and Daddy watered the stock, while Maisie checked each for dehydration.

Sometime after midday, a wind barreled in from the west and blew around even more sand. We sat huddled under the wagons, covered in blankets from head to toe, feeling choked and exhausted, until about dusk when it blew itself out. Shaking off the blankets, we stumbled to our feet, only to realize our cows had scattered, and Budweiser was missing.

We saddled the six remaining horses, helped Maisie and Nellie harness the oxen, and split up to search. Greg and Ken rode northwest, Daddy and I backtracked along the trail, and Jesse and James turned south. We had agreed to search for only one hour before returning. Maisie and Nellie would use the cooling temperature and fading light of dusk to move on southwest along the trail.

After an hour, Daddy and I turned and headed back. We arrived first. Soon afterward, Ken and Greg returned. We were discussing leaving the buckboard or using one of the horses to pull it when James and Jessie returned with three cows, one of them the calf, and Budweiser.

"Found them near an alkali pool, not much water, and the cows may have drunk from it. All around were dead animals and bones. Some of which were human," Jesse said.

"Greg, is there any water in the buckboard?" James asked.

"Yeah, a couple of bladders full and a basin. I'll help," he replied.

I led Budweiser over first, and after he had his fill, I started harnessing him to the buckboard. All of the cows, except one, drank. We filled our canteens and slowly traveled west to join the wagons. The night turned dark, as clouds often obscured what little light the moon provided. With Clown tied behind, I drove the wagon, shivering in the cold. At least we all had our heavy clothing, but I wished for a blanket. We had traveled for a little over an hour when we heard rifle shots in the distance.

They left me. All five men rode off in the direction of the shots. There I sat, alone. Just me and Budweiser, in the middle of the desert, at night. I didn't think I even had a gun! But, I felt under the seat and came up with the Greener shotgun. I checked. It was loaded. I placed it across my lap and held it with my right hand as I urged Budweiser on.

I don't know how far or how long we traveled, just us two in the desert with no one else in sight, before I heard more shots. It sounded like a real battle. I could pick out the sound of pistols and rifles, including one much louder than the others. I didn't want to risk Budweiser or myself riding into the gun battle, so I pulled him back to a slow walk. At first, the sounds of gunfire were rapid and almost constant. Then the rate of fire slowed and finally stopped. My mind began to go crazy with worry. Who was shooting? Was anyone hurt or dead? Did Indians attack in the desert? Why did they leave me?

Another ten minutes brought me close enough to hear shouting. Suddenly, a man appeared before me, right out of the darkness. A break in the clouds allowed enough moonlight so I could see him clearly, especially the large revolver in his hand.

"Step down from that there wagon, girlie, I'm tired of walking. Looks like you and me goin' a have a little fun. I might even take you with me. when we're done. If you scream, I'll kill you," he demanded, waving the pistol in my direction.

"No," I responded sternly. However, I shook with fear as he grabbed for the reins and pointed that big pistol in my direction.

"I said get down. You won't be so pretty after I beat some of the spunk out of you."

Scared and alone, I pulled back on Budweiser's reins and reached to tie them off with my left hand. Immediately, one more shot rang out from nearby, and the man turned in the direction of the sound. In Annie Oakley style, I raised the shotgun, pulling back on the hammers at the same instant, and fired from the hip. I remember nothing else.

214

Greg here. Finally, I get a chance to tell the story. Rose really can't tell this part because she doesn't remember it. So, here's what happened.

After we all rode off into the night when the first shot rang out, I realized we had left Rose all alone, but I wasn't too worried. I figured she knew about the loaded Greener shotgun under the buckboard seat. What trouble could she get into? She was safer away from the gunfire. Besides, I mean, in a real emergency, she could just jump to 2016.

Anyway, by the time we reached the wagons, we could see Nellie and Maisie hunkered down behind the Jacksons' wagon firing at someone out in the desert. Dad motioned for James and Jesse to go with him, and they started a flanking movement. That left Matthew and me to back up Nellie and Maisie. Ground tying our horses, to keep them from running off—it's something like telling a dog to stay, which is what I did with Boone—Matthew and I crept up to join the fight right as two men rushed the wagons. Maisie took down one, who proceeded to scream, "I'm dying, I'm dying!" The other turned and ran, under heavy fire, away from us and toward those on his flank. The gunfight now centered on Dad, James, and Jesse's side. After reloading and checking on Maisie and Nellie, Matthew and I retrieved our horses, and I placed Boone in the wagon and told him to stay, yet again. Along with being shaken and scared, Nellie was furious.

"How dare those men just shoot at us! Don't they have any manners? We would have given them food and shared our water. I declare," she stammered.

Maisie, on the other hand, had grabbed the first aid box and was trying to staunch the bleeding wound of the man who now only whimpered how he was dying. When Matthew and I approached, she simply shook her head, and raised her hands from the blood-drenched cloth. Matthew took her in his arms and talking softly, calmed her, and dried her tears.

We could, by then, hear only sporadic gun shots. Finally, Dad, James, and Jesse approached. "One got away, headed back down the trail. We're going after him!" Dad yelled.

"Oh, good God, no!" Matthew screamed. "Rose!"

I don't think we had ridden even a quarter mile when we heard the bomb-like blast of the big 12-gauge Greener shotgun. Fancy, a skittish Appaloosa, took to the air and threw Jesse off with one swift move. As I passed him, he bounced to his feet and grabbed her reins. I rode on, figuring he was okay. Dad on Romeo reached the buckboard first with Matthew right behind.

"I need light, damn, I need light," Dad kept yelling.

216

James arrived and pulled out two emergency LED flashlights from his saddle bag. "Always be prepared. Is she hurt?" he asked while grabbing Matthew and pulling him out of Ken's way.

"YES, there's a large lump on her head. I found her slumped in the wagon bed with the shotgun still in her hands. Greg, look around, someone must have made her fire the Greener.? We need to get her back to the wagons and let Maisie have a look at her. Matthew, if she needs treatment, we'll call for EMS."

I grabbed an extra flashlight that James held out to me and began to search the area around the wagon. I could see footprints and spots of blood on the white sand. Then I saw the pistol, just lying beside the wagon wheel.

"Dad, look, it's our Walter Colt. I found it beside the wagon. It must have been the man who hit Mom. I found spots of blood, so Rose did shoot him, but no body. I guess he wandered off."

"Matthew, tie Traitor and climb in. You can hold Rose. I'll drive. Greg, get Romeo. Let's get back; this time we've gone off and left Nellie and Maisie alone. Whomever Rose shot is on his own."

"Nope, Jesse must have gone back to the wagons after getting thrown by Fancy. Notice he's not here with us," I answered.

"Right, smart-thinking young man, but let's not let him ride Fancy again anytime soon," James joked.

Dad and Matthew placed Rose in our wagon and Maisie climbed in to have a look. She also called over Jesse, who is a trained paramedic.

"Matthew, she has a concussion, probably from hitting her head on the buckboard seat. It didn't break the skin, but did make a wee lump on her head. She's awake now. I can ride with her and wake her every thirty minutes. If I see any changes, I'll let Ken know, and we can jump back and call for EMS pickup, but I really doubt that'll be necessary," Maisie explained.

"Truly, Matthew, she'll be fine. Maisie's right, she needs rest and time. I'll check on her often, and if anything changes you'll be the first to know," Jesse said.

"Can I see her?" Matthew asked. I could hear pleading and worry in his voice.

"Sure, Matthew, climb up and sit with her a minute, then drive the wagon. That way you'll be close," Ken urged.

"Greg, you and James round up all the horses and cows and tie each to a wagon or the buckboard, then you and Jesse walk lead, switching off to ride ahead every half hour or so. James, you drive the second wagon. Nellie, can you drive the buckboard? I'll bring up the rear. At least for a while."

"Okay. Are we going to bury those men?" Nellie asked.

"No, Nellie. We need to keep moving. Greg, can you gather up their firearms and see if they had any horses?"

"No need, I already did that, Ken. I found two dead horses by an alkali water hole about 500 yards that away," Jesse said pointing north. "I placed their firearms in the bed of the buckboard."

We rode and walked the whole night, stopping three times to water the livestock. Each time Matthew checked on Rose, he let me know she was sleeping. About an hour after dawn, we encountered soft sand. Hills of sand that slid and slipped under our feet and the wagon wheels. Finally, Dad called a halt. We harnessed all eight oxen to our wagon and pulled it toward the Carson River some three miles away. Then he walked the oxen back, hitched them to the Jacksons' wagon and repeated the trip. Even big Budweiser needed help. We used Romeo and Bridger to help pull while Jesse and I pushed.

Late morning found us at the Carson River with all three wagons, all of our horses, but down to two cows. One died not long before we hit the sand hills. We left her lying dead beside the trail.

At least the Forty Mile Desert was behind us.

Sierra Nevada Mountains from Cloud's Rest
looking southeast to Mt. Clark,
Keystone View Company

23
Mountains

The next day, we proceeded across the Great Basin and entered a small tent village called Ragtown on the Carson River. Only a few wood plank buildings stood among numerous tents housing various traders dealing in hay, water, horses, oxen, and almost all other goods needed by weary travelers. Not needing anything of this sort, we proceeded up the Carson River on a decent road, at least in most places. The Carson River started out as a dirty stream, but by midday the water began to clear.

After another day, Rose returned to good health, except for occasionally having nightmares causing her to scream out in fear. Maisie, who slept in the Harrisons' wagon with her, was then called upon to calm her fears and help her back to sleep. In the daytime, Rose never once mentioned the incident in the desert, and neither did the rest of us.

We chose the Johnson Cutoff or Placerville Route into California. From Ragtown, we headed west along the Carson River. The river created an oasis of sorts across the remainder of the Great Basin. Not until we reached the area where Carson City is today did we arrive at the base of the mountains. As we climbed higher into the Carson Range, the river held fresh, clean cold water. Soon, a grassy valley provided all we needed, so we camped for a day to allow our oxen to recover from the desert crossing.

Now we had to traverse the dreaded Sierra Nevadas, and the date was the 7th of October. Snow might have already fallen in the mountains, but most accounts Rose had read and the STTIU had researched, said the trail could be used most of the winter for horse travel. Who knew if wagons could make the crossing? For the next ninety miles or so, we needed all of our wits and strength. First, we crossed the Carson Range by following Cold Creek and then turned south along Lake Tahoe. There we encountered an occasional bit of swampy ground near the lake's edge. It was almost like driving the wagons through deep sand, only this time everything became cold and wet.

At the southern end of the lake, we turned due west toward Echo Summit or Johnson's Pass. Here we encountered snow, at first only a few inches. As we climbed higher and higher, the snow became deeper and deeper. Sometimes, we encountered deep gorges filled with snow. Other gorges would have only a few inches.

Each day we plodded on and on. Rarely making more than ten miles a day, some days we covered only five miles and fell into our bedrolls exhausted with the effort. We broke a double tree on the approach to Johnson's Pass and lost almost a whole day making repairs. The following day, we broke several spokes on the front wheel of the Jacksons' wagon. For every inch of our journey, we had carried a spare in the buckboard. Had we not done so, we would have needed to leave the Jacksons' wagon behind. Another day passed as we set the replacement wheel in place.

At night, we could bundle into our sleeping bags and stay fairly warm. Right before we started up the mountains, Dad called for a supply run from headquarters. We all needed warm boots. Rose seemed particularly happy to get hers and found them stuffed with colorful, warm woolen socks. She shared them with Maisie, Baidepe, and Nellie. During the day, we used blankets, and even our sleeping bags when we could, to keep warm. Fresh game became scarce, but unknown to me (and possibly others), headquarters had stocked our supplies with lots of ready-to-eat meals that only needed heating.

"Greg, I know we're doing this so the Jacksons can reach California with Baidepe, but don't you think it's cheating? Are we really getting the true pioneer experience?" Rose asked one day as we rode side by side after having hot beef stew for lunch.

"What!?! I've been doing this since June! Almost four months! I almost drowned while crossing a river, and I have eaten enough salt bacon and beans to last a lifetime. I may not want to time travel for years, especially to this period," I shouted with attitude.

"Oh, just checking," she replied laughing. "But still, I wonder how much worse this could get if we didn't have along such modern conveniences."

Johnson's Pass brought us to the descent portion of the mountains. We had climbed to some 7,400 feet, and now we needed to go back down. Pulling the wagons uphill was dangerous and tough on our oxen. Going down created a new set of problems. The first and most important problem was keeping our wagons' speed down. If the wagons moved too fast, they would push the falling tongue, to which the oxen were harnessed, causing them to stumble or fall. Additionally, the trail often ran along side steep cliffs, where one side was sheer rock and the other a straight drop into open space.

Of course, that's also when we encountered the first serious snow. It began during the night and continued for three days straight. Wet, heavy snow blanketed everything. We managed to make about five miles the first day west of the pass. We camped for one cold, long day, keeping our livestock close by and melting snow for water frequently. The next day, we traveled a bit farther down the mountains. This often meant walking ahead of the wagons to even find the trail. Upon encountering a sheltered place near dusk, we camped and waited out the storm. Luckily it blew out early the next morning. With the end of the snowstorm, the temperature fell to below freezing and probably below zero.

The heavy snowfall meant our oxen had to work even harder. Up small rises, around sharp bends, and down ice-slicked passages we moved, sometimes inch by inch. The third day west of the summit, we awoke to find the calf dead and mostly frozen. We were all surprised he had made it this far.

Maisie and Jesse cleaned snow and ice from the horses' and oxen's hooves several times each day. Nellie kept the chickens warm by covering them with an extra layer of blankets and keeping them in their wagon. Finally, we decided they wouldn't last much longer, and we devoured fried chicken and roasted chicken for breakfast and dinner. The next day, our last cow slid on the ice and fell over a cliff. While we regretted her death, it taught us all a lesson about being very careful on icy patches of rock.

Finally, on the first day of November 1853, we reached a mining settlement called Hangtown, now Placerville, California. We knew the town was rough and a bit lawless. We camped on the outskirts, staying near the American River that we had mostly followed for the last few weeks. The weather settled in at about 60 degrees during the day. It felt almost like summer.

Our party now split into many pieces. Maisie returned to Scotland and her veterinarian practice. Rose and Matthew decided to stay with James and Nellie, as did Jesse. The plan was for them to move west to Sacramento and then continue northward for about a week along the Sacramento River. There, on the river, waiting for them stood a log and plank house and about one hundred acres of land, already registered in James' name. Here they planned to raise horses, some cattle, and Baidepe. The STTIU had purchased the land and built the house. The little town near their ranch was called Red Bluff. It even had a post office. Not that it would do us any good.

On our last day together, Rose hesitated and then asked me, "Greg, you haven't ever mentioned your soon-to-be baby sister. Have you thought of what they might name her?"

"It's a girl?"

"Of course, it's a girl. I told you that day back at Fort Bridger, the day we found you, silly."

"Oh, I didn't remember."

"Hasn't your mother mentioned the baby when you talk to her at night?"

"Not really, I think she was waiting for me to bring it up. And, well . . . I just haven't. I ask her each time how she's feeling, but well . . . I don't know how to talk about the baby."

"Really, Greg, it's not an alien! You just ask. Remember – use your words."

"Okay, I'll ask her tonight, when we get home. I can tell you later this week when we call."

24
Home

So Dad and I jumped to our time and flew home. Dad was anxious about Mom, and she wouldn't let me stay in 1853 without him. Mom really looked like she was going to have a baby, and soon! I made the mistake of pointing this out. Hint: never, ever, tell any woman her stomach is huge!

Dad and I settled back into ranch life. Winter came on strong, and I spent a lot of time catching up on school work, reading books, and watching television. I did miss Rose, but at least I had Boone and Becky.

Rose and Matthew returned just before Christmas. James, Nellie, and Baidepe were settled and making plans for the coming year.

In January, two important things happened. The first really good, as Mom gave birth to a tiny baby girl on January 2nd. They named her Kara Louise. *Kara* after a special friend of theirs from about 3,000 years ago, and *Louise*, which is Nellie's middle name. You should have seen my Dad, he re-learned how to change diapers, clean up spit-up, and even give her a bath. He walked the floor with her when she had colic and even sang to her!

Late in January, Nellie received word she really had won a big prize for one of her novels. She returned briefly to our time and accepted her award. Dad helped her spend the money on some really good mares, as Nellie knows little about horses. She also bought gifts and books for Baidepe and James. I got to go with her to deliver the horses to their ranch. We took Midnight along. Dad rushed back home to be with Mom and Kara.

When we arrived at their ranch, I discovered *Baidepe* actually meant *daughter* in Nez Perce. The girl we had called Baidepe for all those months had finally told them about being captured with her mother from a Nez Perce village and traded many, many months later to the Pawnee. She never talked about the raid on the village that had killed her mother, but did finally tell them her name—*Peopeo*, it means little bird. I noticed James, more often than not, called her Baidepe.

Rose and I spent the rest of the winter and on until late spring catching up on our school work. Since Rose continued to have nightmares, a counselor came to the ranch every other week and spent the night. I talked with him as well. I'd had the same dream about drowning over and over again and found it hard to get to sleep. It took months, but slowly, we both came to terms with our misadventures in 1853. Since our return, neither one of us has time traveled much, and never alone. We did go and see Nellie and James. We all visited in late spring and spent a week at their ranch, helping with various chores and just having fun in 1854.

Epilogue

It's been about a year and a half since our adventures on the trail. Much has happened. First, Rose and I wrote our narratives about our 1853 adventure. Nellie helped me self-publish my first three adventures, although Rose says the name of the third book is wrong, as it is her adventures as well as mine. I did put her down as a co-author. Anyway, we hope to publish this narrative real soon.

Rose and Matthew have gone to Scotland to see Maisie twice. She and Holly have visited us once. We also went to New York to see Holly perform in *Swan Lake*. Rose called it romantic. I'll have to admit, Holly is an amazing dancer.

Kara is now walking and talking. Boone and Becky, who now seems to belong to Rose, herd Kara constantly, which most often makes her scream out in frustration when she can't go where she wants to. More often than not, the two dogs are keeping her safe and away from stairs, horses, oxen, and snakes. I take Kara for horseback rides in the summer. Rose is teaching her colors and numbers. Kara time traveled with us when we went to see James and Nellie, but never on her own, as far as we can tell.

We have a new housekeeper, cook, and teacher, Mary. She cooks better than Mom, but not as good as Nellie. I've grown two inches and am now 6' 3". Rose is still only 5' 2". I like to tease her about being over a foot shorter than me.

Dad returned to work. He mostly works with Jesse now, who took James' position at STTIU. In late June, Dad and James planned to testify at the Pirate's trial. The day before Dad was to leave for Washington, D.C., the STTIU director called and asked for Dad. About an hour later, he called us all into the living room.

After waiting for us all to turn and stop talking, Dad stated, "the director called to let me know personally that the Pirate and his accomplice have both escaped."

"How?" we all yelled.

"Seems they were brought into the STTIU courtroom for a pretrial hearing. Both were seated at the defendant's table, along with John. Suddenly three people, supposedly there for a later hearing, threw them each a coin. The Pirate and his accomplice, whose real names we still don't know, caught theirs and jumped. The three people in the audience also jumped. Fortunately, John didn't catch the one thrown to him, and he remains under strict guard. His trial has been postponed."

Dad and Jesse are still hunting for the Pirate.

What's True?

It is my intent to write history as I understand it, without any prejudice against any race or religion. I spend months researching before even beginning to write each book. I do not wish to "whitewash" history. I try to be factual and to place my story in as accurate a background as possible.

Some parents may be upset by my presentation of firearms in these stories. I understand your concerns and respect your opinion; however, the use of weapons, in particular firearms in my stories, is accurate. While I do not advocate allowing children to use firearms, I recognize their use and their necessity in some historical periods.

Rebecca Ketcham traveled from Ithaca, New York, to Oregon in 1853 with William H. Gray's party and a large number of sheep. She was in her mid-to-late teens. She was not related to any of the other members of the party. She did often ride side-saddle on what she called a "bay pony" each day. Gray used herding dogs to protect and herd the sheep. Rebecca kept a journal which was published by the

Oregon Historical Society in their quarterly journal in 1961. It can be found at http://www.jstor.org/.

Amelia Jenks Bloomer (May 27, 1818 – December 30, 1894) was an American women's rights and temperance advocate who took to wearing the Bloomer Suit in the mid-1850s. She believed the "costume of women should be suited to her wants and necessities. It should conduce at once to her health, comfort, and usefulness; and, while it should not fail also to conduce to her personal adornment, it should make that end of secondary importance." Fanny Kemble, an actress and author of the period, and Elizabeth Cady Stanton, a women's suffrage advocate, both wore bloomers at various times.

Joel Hembree's grave can be found about ¼ mile to the west of its original setting on private land, next to the grave of Private Ralston Baker, killed in an Indian skirmish on May 1, 1867. The original headstone was placed on Hembree's new grave.

Joel Jordan Hembree, his wife Sara (Sally) and their eight sons from McMinnville, Tennessee, were part of the estimated 1,000 men, women and children who left Fitzhugh's Mill near Independence, Missouri, in May 1843, for Oregon. On July 18, between Bed Tick Creek and LaPrele Creek, six-year-old Joel Hembree, the second youngest son, fell from the wagon tongue on which he was riding and was fatally injured. Diarist William T. Newby wrote, July 18: "A very bad road. Joel J. Hembrees son Joel fel off the waggeon tung & both wheels run over him.

Distance 17 miles. July 19: Lay buy. Joel Hembree departed this life about 2 o'clock. July 20: We buried the youth & ingraved his name on the headstone." Dr. Marcus Whitman described the fatality as "a wagon having passed over the abdomen." This is the oldest identified grave along the Oregon Trail.

Joel's body, originally buried 1/4 mile east, was moved March 24, 1962 and placed beside Pvt. Ralston Baker, who was killed in an Indian skirmish on 1 May 1867, near the site of the 1860's LaPrele Stage and Pony Express station. Learn more at: http://wyoshpo.state.wy.us/trailsdemo/hembreebaker.htm.

The State of Wyoming has a great website about the **Sweetwater River** crossings at http://wyoshpo.state.wy.us/trailsdemo/threecrossings.htm.

You can learn more about the **Donner Party** at https://www.history.com/topics/donner-party.

American Indians rarely attacked wagon trains in the early years of the Westward Expansion. Diaries and letters of the period show such attacks were quite rare, although Indians often stole horses and cattle. By the late 1850s, attacks became more common, mainly because the heavy settlement of the west by whites caused the Indians to fight back to retain their own hunting grounds and resources.

Mormons at Fort Bridger - A well-written history of these events and the tension between Jim

Bridger and the Mormons can be found at https://www.wyohistory.org/encyclopedia/fort-bridger.

Ward Massacre - Boise, Idaho - This brutal attack is best described at https://www.theclio.com/web/entry?id=23713.

Want to see someone actually **hitch oxen** to a wagon? This might even be where Ken learned to do it! Check out https://www.youtube.com/watch?v=Xc5UfHwNgxA at the Lincoln Log Cabin State Historic site.

Two excellent **maps of our nation's westward expansion** can be found at: https://www.nps.gov/oreg/planyourvisit/maps.htm and https://www.nps.gov/cali/planyourvisit/maps.htm. Both can be enlarged and printed.

Glossary

Apple Pan Dowdy: an old New England dessert, pan dowdy is similar to skillet apple pie. The top crust is pressed or slashed into the apples so that the juices flood over and caramelize the top crust.

Buffalo chips: the dried dung of buffalo used as fuel, especially by early settlers.

Bowie knife: a fixed-blade fighting knife created by James Black in the early 19th century for Jim Bowie, who had become famous for his use of a large knife. Jim Bowie died at the Alamo.

Cabinet card: a mid-nineteenth century photograph mounted on sturdy card stock

Hemp: a plant used for making cloth and rope

Linseed oil: an oil obtained from flaxseed

Meander: to flow in a winding or indirect course

Monolith: an extremely large single piece of stone

Rain shadow: the area to the lee of mountains, it receives less rainfall than the area windward of the mountains.

Rancheros: Mexican cowboys

Scree field: a steep hillside covered with rocks, sometimes called a talus slope, caused by glacial flow

Tributary: a stream or body of water that flows into a larger body of water

Windlass: a wench used for for raising or hauling objects

About the Author
C.M. Huddleston

C.M. Huddleston won gold medals for *Greg's First Adventure in Time* and *Greg's Second Adventure in Time* from Literary Classics in 2016 and 2017 respectively. She has been an elementary school teacher, an archaeologist, an historian, an historic preservation consultant, and a writer.

C.M. Huddleston endeavors to make all of her book's historical settings and events accurate and realistic. Of course, we humans can't yet time travel, but she's hoping *you* can in your life time! Just imagine the adventures you can have.

Learn more about Greg and his coming adventures in time travel at www.cmhuddleston.com. Also, C.M. Huddleston wrote two short stories about Greg and Rose for the award-winning anthology *Winter Wonder.*

Teachers and home school instructors, you can find activities and lessons related to all of C.M. Huddleston's Adventure in Time books at www.cmhuddleston.com/lesson-plans.html.